Praise for Val M

"*A Time Outworn* is a first novel, a delicate, sensitive melancholy one written in a cool and lovely prose ..."
Orville Prescott, *New York Times*

"*A Peacock Cry* has more of the mind than the heart ... a readable, adult novel ... the writing taut and economical."
R.G., *The Irish Times*

"Character is very exactly caught ... and one of the most potenent presences is Ireland herself, potent, volatile ... "
Jacky Gillott, *The Times*

Feeling, knowledge and talent layered tight like feathers on a wing ..."
Polly Devlin, *Vogue*

"Her style is hard and perfect, and she has given us a considerable achievement to reckon with."
Benedict Kiely

" ... 'Memory and Desire', one of the finest stories to have been published in Ireland for many years."
Colm Tóibín, *In Dublin*

"These beautiful stories so composed they border on a very special Mulkernsian wildness. A masterly writer in the tradition of Seán Ó Faoláin".
Sebastian Barry

By the same author

A Time Outworn
A Peacock Cry
Antiquities
An Idle Woman
The Summerhouse
A Friend of Don Juan
Very Like A Whale

ABOUT THE AUTHOR

Val Mulkerns is an Irish writer and member of Aosdána. Her first novel, *A Time Outworn*, was released to critical acclaim in Ireland in 1951. She was associate editor and theatre critic for *The Bell* later worked as a journalist and columnist and is often heard on the radio. She is the author of four novels, three collections of short stories, two children's books and many published essays and critical writings. In 1953 she married Maurice Kennedy and they have two sons and a daughter.

A third edition of her 1984 novel, *The Summerhouse* was published in 2013 and her memoir, *Friends With The Enemy* will be published in 2017. She lives in Dublin, Ireland.

For more information please see:

www.valmulkerns.com

MEMORY
AND
DESIRE

VAL MULKERNS

451
Editions

Memory and Desire, First Edition, 2016

Published by 451 Editions
Dublin and New York
www.451editions.com

© Val Mulkerns 2016

The stories were originally published in *Antiquities*
(André Deutsch, 1978), *An Idle Woman* (Poolbeg Press,
1980) and *A Friend of Don Juan* (John Murray, 1988)

ISBN: 978-0-9931443-1-8

Cover and interior design: www.Cyberscribe.ie
Cover painting by Louise Newman: www.louisenewman.ie
From the collection of David Larkin: www.haddington.ie

Printed in Ireland by SPRINT-print Ltd

Table of Contents

MEMORY AND DESIRE

Special Category

When his number was called for a visit he couldn't quite believe it. His was not a travelling family although they were all involved one way or another with the railway. When the sergeant came rattling the keys he was not on his feet as presumably most of the other lucky prisoners were, but still sitting on the edge of his bed, hands dangling between his knees, wondering who could possibly have managed to cross over and see him. Money was scarce at home and they might come to bury him but not otherwise.

"Get a move on there, Foxy," the sergeant said without rancour. "Or maybe you'd care to comb out the foxy head before the barber blows in one of these days. You won't have the hair long then, my lad, and we'll have to think up another name for ye, won't we? Name such as Skinny or summat." His wheezy laugh was obviously well meant. This small red-nosed man was not the worst, not malicious like the tall good-looking sergeant who always singled him out for special baiting. The heavy coppery hair which had given B323 his family nickname seemed to annoy authority wherever he went, even before all this. It was difficult perhaps to look dutiful and dependable with a head of hair that flickered as though a searchlight were perpetually playing on it, that sprang into an imperial helmet of curls at the first touch of rain.

Now however in the yard where the prisoners exercised the sun beat down, stinging his eyes after the gloom of his cell. The sky was the same blue that had hardly darkened at all even when stars shone over the barricades during the fight. But that must be months ago now. He felt a little sleepy in the fresh air, unwilling to make the effort to look along the line of faces on the other side of the rough fencing to find his visitor. Finally B323 made an effort and ran his eye swiftly over the assembled faces, embarrassed or happy or shining with tears, none of them remotely familiar faces. His was not a visiting family, he reminded himself once again. He made an appeal to the red-nosed sergeant.

"Take me back, please, there's been some mistake. I know nobody here."

"Sir," the sergeant said.

"I know nobody here, sir."

"Daft little foxy bastard," the sergeant said amiably, although he was more than a foot shorter than the prisoner. "There's been no bleeding mistake. Show ye."

He left the line of military with fixed bayonets and went along the row of visitors, checking permits. B323 saw him stop and joke with a pretty girl in a straw boater with summery ribbons dangling between blue cotton shoulders. The gay dog made her laugh and shake her long hair, and then he returned to the only prisoner who hadn't found his visitor.

"Git over there, Foxy," the sergeant said. "Don't ye

know your luck when ye see it? Nice little bit o' fluff she is too. Go over there and try her." Baffled, the tall fiery prisoner walked over to the line of visitors and saw that the girl's eyes were speckled blue as a bird's egg and she was laughing again.

"Hello, Bartholomew Mullens. You're not a bit like I thought you'd be."

"I'm sorry, but neither are you. My brother Paddy looks quite different."

He had forgotten the sound of a girl's laugh, so he tried to make her laugh again. It was easy.

"I thought Bartholomew Mullens had to be small and spotty with a large Adam's apple and a very nice nature," she said. "I thought Bartholomew Mullens would have no way with the ladies and that I'd have to talk to him about his interests – butterfly catching, maybe, or stamp collecting, or the lives of the saints, or how nice it used to be down on his auntie's farm before he heard of Mother Ireland."

"I never had an auntie with a farm, I'm sorry to say, and nobody ever calls me anything except – except Red Mull." She laughed so loudly at this that her elderly neighbour in black touched the girl's arm in reproof and put a finger to her lips. "Sorry." The girl giggled quietly then, before looking up at him under her summery hat. "I'm Frances Montgomery from Dublin. And I have an auntie with a farm – here in Cheshire – who asked me over for a holiday."

"But you haven't told me how you came to know my name?"

"I read the list of prisoners in *The Irish Times* book

just before I came over. And I thought, poor Bartholomew Mullens, a boy with a name like that needs to be cheered up. When I saw you were in Knutsford I knew it was near where I was going so I wrote to the Governor and said I was your cousin and asked permission to visit you."

"You're not a member of Cumann na mBan then?"

"Oh no, nothing like that. My mother would ask for her smelling salts at the mention of them. But my father's a bit of a rebel, always was. He gave me Mitchel's *Jail Journal* to read when I was ten and I've never been able to forget it. Have you ever read it?"

"If I hadn't I don't think I'd be here," the prisoner said unguardedly, and to his consternation her eyes filled with tears, which she quickly blinked away. "Also of course I saw William Butler Yeats's play *Cathleen Ni Houlihan*."

"I saw it too in the Abbey Theatre," the girl said eagerly, "and when Michael went out after the Poor Old Woman I wanted to go with him. But next day I didn't. I wrote a poem about it instead."

"Would you show it to me?"

"I might if you showed me some of yours."

"How do you know I've written any?"

"Everyone of our age in Dublin writes poetry. Father says that's what's wrong with the country these days. Did anything you wrote get printed?"

He felt himself go red as his hair, and she pounced on this admission. Where was it printed, could she get copies?

"It was nothing," he said at last. "A few parodies covered book that sold for sixpence. Some of them also were printed in broadsheets. I set the verses to popular

14

airs you could march to. They were supposed to be funny."

"Could I get the book when I go back home? Could I buy it in Eason's?"

"Maybe. The publisher was the Art Depot in Mary Street – if Eason's haven't got it, the publishers might have a few copies left."

"A poet," she said, flatteringly awed. "A poet who's been printed."

"Now will you show me your poems?"

"I'll write to you when I get back home if I may, and I'll copy some out. The best one, anyway. Will they let you have letters?"

"I don't know, he said. "I haven't had any yet. I'll try to find out."

"Father said it was a *poet's rebellion*," the girl remembered suddenly. "Professor McDonagh and Patrick Pearse and Joseph Mary Plunkett. And now Bartholomew Mullins."

"Do you know where they are now?" he said, smiling at his name tagged on among his betters. "I never really found out for certain because we are not allowed newspapers and I've been in solitary for so long."

"You mean you don't know?"

"The last time they asked me to sign the paper, they said people who wouldn't sign would be shot, but I didn't believe them."

"This must be the promise to be of good conduct in future, and not to impede the war effort and so on?"

So this much was known outside? "Yes." He became aware for the first time of the other visitors around them, perhaps because the girl looked uneasy, as though she would like to go. The bell clanged out through the hot summer afternoon.

"I must go or maybe they won't let me come again," she said, dipping her hand suddenly into the carpet bag at her feet.

"Goodbye, Miss Montgomery, you are very good to come."

"Please call me Fanny. I don't expect these cigarettes are the right brand or anything but maybe you could swap them. The rest of the stuff might be useful if you get hungry between meals. Jacob's biscuits from home."

To his astonishment she smiled coaxingly as she put a big brown paper bag into his hands and was gone before he could thank her. But she hadn't answered his question and even as he called her she was running back.

"They shot Patrick Pearse with two others on the third of May. I remember because it was my birthday."

"And the rest of the leaders?"

"They shot all the signatories of the Proclamation – on different days at the end of April and early May."

"Connolly too? We heard at the barricades he was badly hurt."

"Connolly too," she said. "I'll come to see you again, Red Mull, if they let me."

"God go with you, Fanny. Don't forget the poem, will you?"

"I won't forget but it's not good. Remember it was I who said it." And she was gone. The last he saw of her was the back of the straw hat with its tossing ribbons among the dark clothes of the other women.

Almost at once the red-nosed sergeant was at his side. "Told ye she was a nice little bit o' fluff, Foxy, didden

I?" he whispered. "Open up the dibs, there, till we see wot she brought yer. Blimey, bloody millionaires she must come from. Player's Navy Cut – a whole bloody box o' smokes – Fry's creamy chocolate and Jacob's biscuits. Some blokes 'as all the luck, Foxy me lad."

"If you come to my cell tonight you can have your share of all this, sergeant. I suppose the bag has to be inspected now for hand grenades or something?"

"Ye never knows yer luck – might be allowed keep the lot, Foxy. But I doubt it."

"Meaning what?"

"Meaning tuck and that is for chappies as signs their paper, see? You said no, Foxy, four times by all I hear."

"That's right, sergeant. And I'll continue to say no."

"Well, same as I said, ye never knows yer luck. Quick march now, look sharp."

At the entrance to the prisoner's own block, the bag was taken away from him and he was told he might have some of the contents returned to him later. The block officer scribbled the prisoner's number on the outside of the bag. B323, followed by a question mark.

"I request permission, sir, to smoke one of those cigarettes now." Even as he heard himself speaking, he despised himself.

"Permission refused."

"I request permission then for pencil and paper."

"Permission also refused. Return the prisoner to his quarters, sergeant."

"Yes, sir."

Before the cell door clanged behind him the sergeant whispered. "Do wot I can for ye later, Foxy."

Dead, all dead.

Connolly and Pearse and McDonagh and McBride and Plunkett and Clarke and Eamon Ceannt. All dead, while he bent the knee to the extent of asking for a lousy cigarette. He sat on the edge of his plank bed and watched his hands shaking.

For a few days death was far away from the adventure of Cuckoo Lane. Death was distant gunfire magnified by the golden air and the full river opposite the Four Courts. A shell which had burst in O'Connell Street (they were told) bounced in successive waves of sound under the four bridges and then seemed to explode in diamonds against the river wall. But nobody suffered more than sore eardrums. The dead were somewhere else. The small company of men left briefly in his charge by Commandant Daly had laughed like schoolboys (which two of them were) when he sang his own parody for them – "Come Along and Join the British Army". They were tired and dirty but not sleepy, although most of them had had no sleep for four nights. The girls billeted in the nearby Father Matthew Hall had looked after them well, and being a soldier was something new and interesting after the routine of normal life.

Sometimes on the night watch he was back in brief waves of weariness on the footplate of his engine, watching the golden showers of sparks that flew like a shaken flag in the night sky when he opened the refuelling hatch on the long dark trip to Galway. Shovelling coal, his face black, he often laughed then to think of his other very private life, the elocution lessons he paid for out of what his mother left him from his wages, the Irish lessons at the Conradh office in Parnell Square, the dizzy day he was auditioned for the Abbey Theatre when the poet said, "Interesting what you have managed to do with the voice of a callow young student from Trinity, Mr Fay," and Mr Fay replied, pleased. "This is not the student, Mr Yeats. This is a young fireman from the Midland and Great Western Railway – he never went beyond the seventh book, but as you see he met the scholars coming home. He writes songs too."

They exchanged a little laugh. "He might do for Michael, don't you think, if the other boy can't attend rehearsals," Mr Yeats said, "and this remarkable red hair would look well on stage."

"I was hoping you'd say that. The red hair would indeed be right," Mr Fay replied. They spoke as if he weren't there but he didn't mind that. In the end he did play Michael for a whole week, and maybe it was that which decided him about joining the Volunteers. The frightening silence of the theatre, the wave of emotion that broke over the packed bodies he couldn't see, excited him like wine as he waited for his cue from Miss Allgood's breathtaking lines every night.

> *Many that are red-cheeked now will be pale-cheeked; many that have been free to walk the hills and the bogs and the rushes will be sent to walk hard streets in far countries; many a good plan will be broken; many that have gathered money will not stay to spend it; many a child will be born and there will be no father at its christening to give it a name. They that have red*

cheeks will have pale cheeks for my sake, and for
all that they will think they are well paid.
They shall be remembered for ever.
They shall be alive for ever …

Somewhere between the theatre and the red footplate in the darkness the desire to follow Tone and Mitchel and fight for his country was born and he knew why he was never for a moment affected by the recruiting posters all over the city: "Your Country Needs YOU." His country perhaps did need him, but his country wasn't England. It was a shadowy place the speeches of Patrick Pearse and the journal of John Mitchel and the heady lines of William Butler Yeats had suddenly brought very close. It was Inis Ealga or Banba or Fodhla, and its queen had big eyes that blazed like Maud Gonne's. There were some that called her the Poor Old Woman and there were some who called her Cathleen the daughter of Houlihan.

At the barricades in Cuckoo Lane he knew his job in the railway was gone for ever and that his family might even disown a member so foolish as to disemploy himself in these hard times, but he didn't care. He didn't see any further than the starry April sky that was soft like summer and the comradeship that was like nothing he had ever known before. A thin girl of whom Fanny Montgomery reminded him used to come with food for them from the Father Matthew Hall. He was always worried that a stray bullet might kill or injure her on her way over to Cuckoo Lane and one night he told her so, offering to ask Commandant Daly if he might convey her back. She laughed at him.

20

"Every time I get safely over and back to the Hall I get a great big thrill out of it," she said, and he knew then that she reacted as he did to the great adventure. When it was over he couldn't believe that only six days had passed since the night he packed his kit bag in the kitchen at home after his family had gone to bed. In the farewell note to his mother he had said, "Don't worry about me – this is why I was born and I've never been more content. God keep you all till I see you again when we've taught John Bull a lesson and set old Ireland free. In case of a raid, burn this letter from your loving son, Red Mull."

She wasn't like the schoolboy's mother who had come to the barricades and shamed him in front of the men, begging him to come home before he got killed. She wasn't like the student's mother who had brought him a change of clothes and passed it through the railings of the Rotunda Gardens where they had lain all night after surrender. She wasn't like the rossies who had sniggered under their shawls when the band of dirty beaten men who were his comrades staggered out next morning into the sunshine of shattered O'Connell Street opposite Crane's Musical Emporium.

"A fine pack of chocolate soldiers youse are to be freeing oul' Ireland – Jasus, would you look at the cut of the Irish Volunteers!' a brassy young one had called out, and for the first time he and his companions had looked at one another. Tired eyes, dusty clothes, week-old beards, stiff and aching limbs through which they tried to get the blood moving again. A fine pack of chocolate soldiers indeed, but spurred by their own dismal appearance they had marched smartly enough to the Richmond Barracks. In the gymnasium they were told to lie down on the floor and then the identification by Dublin G-men began. One by one, as the long hot day wore on, the important prisoners were weeded out: Joe McGuinness, Eamon Duggan, Ned Daly, J. J. Walsh, Dinny O'Callaghan and the old Fenian signatory, Tom Clarke.

Neither to these men nor to anybody else was food or drink offered, and beside him Mullens remembered the sick moaning of the schoolboy who had refused to go home with his mother.

"If only I had a sup of water, Mullens," the boy kept whimpering over and over again and at last he could stand it no longer but wriggled unseen as a snake past man after man until he reached an open window. It was dusky now, but still warm, and underneath a sentry passed and repassed with clicking heels along the yard. Under cover of a few men who saw what he was doing, Mullens leaned over the windowsill.

"Could you get me a cup of water, please, Tommy, for a sick man," he said softly, and the sentry just as softly cursed the seed and breed of all bloody Fenian Paddies. In the end he agreed to a bucketful for two shillings, with a cup thrown in, and Mullens's only fear was that the water would never last as far as the schoolboy. Men whose lips were sore and cracked with thirst clawed at the bucket as it passed. A change of guard made it possible for other deals to be made however with the Tommies in the yard and soon the thirst at least of everybody was quenched. It was to be hours later before the oblong hard dog biscuits were offered to them and by then their fate had been sealed.

22

Come along and join the British Army
Show that you're not afraid
Put your name upon the roll of honour
In the Dublin Pals' Brigade.
We'll send you out to die in France or Belgium
'Twill prove that you are true blue,
When the war is over
If we want you any more
We'll find you in the SDU.

The men had urged him to sing for them as they rocked jam-packed to transportation in the old Slieve Bloom. A soldier had tried to batten down the hatches before she set sail but Mullens had spoken up. "If you want us to survive to be properly chastised, Tommy, that's not the way." The men roared in approval, and later an officer checked the situation and ordered the hatches to be left open.

"Give us a few bars there, Mullser, one of your own," somebody shouted as they pulled out into Dublin Bay, so he led them in singing one of his parodies. Once a song of his had been sung in the Queen's Music Hall and he had been delighted but never thought he might be paid money for such things: he had no idea how the little published collection was faring. He could write better ones now if he could only get his hands on paper and pencil, but that had been refused for months now. He thought of paper with the same greed as he thought of food when he was hungry (which was almost always). He thought of fat lined copybooks and scribbling pads and pads of coloured notepaper and the comforting fat feel of a pencil between his fingers, his favourite kind of pencil which couldn't be rubbed out, a copying ink pencil that turned purple when you spat on it. But any pencil would do, or any broken-down N pen, any half-dried powdery ink. If they'd allow him writing materials he could endure the lack of books and newspapers. Without either and totally without news of home, he sometimes felt like beating his head off the wall.

Since it was clear from what the girl had said that lists of some kind had been published, why hadn't any of his family written to him? They had been against all this of course, thought it criminally neglectful of a son to risk the loss of his job or the loss to them of thirty shillings out of his two pound wage packet, but he didn't think they would go so far as not to write to him. Not his mother anyway. When he went on his holidays – for which he wasn't paid and had to save – she was content with only a pound a week from him to be paid her before going away. Plenty of parents, he knew demanded the usual lot, holidays or no holidays.

A key sounded suddenly in the lock, and he knew from the thickened blue light behind his barred window that it must be supper time. It wasn't, however. The good-looking, swarthy sergeant had come to pay a visit, a sheet of paper in his hand. The prisoner got reluctantly to his feet.

"Good evening, sir," the sergeant prompted.

"Good evening."

The prisoner shrugged as though at a tiresome child and mimicked the exact tone. The blow across the mouth was only moderately painful, being expected.

"I can loan you a pen, B323, which is a lot more than you deserve."

"I'm much obliged to you, sir. If you could prolong the loan and manage a little paper as well I'd regard it as a great favour. I've been asking for both since I came here, sir."

"The only paper you need is in my hand. If you don't sign, I'm instructed to leave you without supper – and by the same token, without any benefit from your food parcel tonight. If you do sign, there's 'am and heggs waiting in the galley. You can be off tomorrow at dawn with a one-way ticket home in your pocket. Sign here, please."

The sergeant bent his handsome oiled black head and drew out the triangular table which was bracketed to the wall.

"Sit down, B323. Make yourself at home."

"No thank you, sir. I've already stated my reasons for not wishing to sign."

"Read the bleedin' paper again, you stubborn Irish bastard, and see that it's a reasonable exchange for your freedom."

"I'll recite the most offensive passage by heart for you, sergeant, if you like."

It wasn't for nothing he'd sweated learning lines between stoking sessions on the footplate. "Being liable to continued detention in internment under the Defence of the Realm Act for the duration of the war, I hereby undertake if released from internment not to engage in any act of a seditious nature or any act calculated to hinder the successful prosecution of the war.' Whose war, sergeant? It's not our war, the Germans were the friends of Ireland. Besides, who is to decide what an act of a 'seditious character' is? Might not playing in one of Mr

Yeats's plays be judged to be one? Signing a paper like this would be signing myself into bondage, not freedom."

"Mere formality," the sergeant said lightly. "That's what your mates think all over the lock-up. Seven more went 'ome today."

"Believe me, I appreciate your concern on my behalf, sir. But there's no change in my attitude."

"There may be a change in ours though, Paddy, see if there mayn't." The threat was accompanied by a final wave of the document in front of his face and the banged iron door left echoes that bounced several times from wall to wall.

When the footsteps died away along the cage walk the prisoner decided he had earned the treat he didn't often allow himself. He bent and picked with his fingers at the flaking whitewash under the place where the table was set into the wall. When you chewed the limey stuff, hunger was baffled after a while and you almost forgot you hadn't eaten. You could spit away what remained in your mouth into the brown porcelain charlie in the corner and pray it would be dissolved in piss before anybody noticed. There was some water in the metal jug still, and he drank that after he'd finished chewing. Tepid dusty stuff it was but it served. There would be nothing better on offer tonight.

He lay down on the bedboards and watched the thickening of the summer light through the bars. If he'd been fed he knew he could have passed the time more pleasurably with forbidden fantasies of girls he knew at home, but now he could think of them only as remote beauties like Mary Pickford or Clara Bow. Somewhere a church bell sounded and somewhere else a dog barked, shrill and prolonged. Barking perhaps for his supper? He would eat slightly fatty scraps of good meat from the family table and maybe some leftover gravy and potatoes. He would maybe finish off with a hard delicious heel of crusty bread and wash it all down with a bowl of cool fresh water. Lucky dog.

Finding a good angle for his shoulder-blades, the prisoner let his mind stray lecherously over visions of food, big plates of fragrant smoked bacon and egg with Hafner's sausages, creamy dishes of tripe and onions, Sunday roasts of rich beef with juice running down the crispy sides to be soaked up in the pan by roasting potatoes, rabbit stew savoury with sage and snowy dumplings, tender pink slices of boiled bacon with green cabbage curling in its juices, and in the centre of the scrubbed table at home a mountain of floury potatoes for the taking, bought in sacks by his driver father in some place like Mullingar or Ballinasloe. Afterwards maybe a spicy apple cake with a frosted sugar garnish or newly baked raisin bread with the golden topping his sister gave it by smearing the round loaves with beaten egg before arranging them in the oven. Then he thought of Frances Montgomery with her summery straw hat and her Jacob's biscuits (what kind? ginger snaps or butter creams or fig rolls, puff cracknels or all sorts of sugar biscuits with brightly coloured tops?) Who would eat her Fry's cream chocolate, from whose lucky mouth would cloud the smoke from her Player's cigarettes?

If he'd had the wit to ask her, she might smuggle him

27

paper and pencil some time and he might get away with it hidden next his skin. But more than likely she'd go home and he'd never see her again. She had told him her father was a journalist on the staff of the *Freeman's Journal* and she lived in a house on the Drumcondra Road near the Bishop's Palace. It wasn't likely he'd ever see her again but he'd never forget her either, herself and her summery hat and her laugh and her Jacob's biscuits. He was almost asleep, almost happy, when the iron key turned in the iron door and he was rasped awake again.

"No more bye-byes, Foxy, got a bitta comfort for ye here." The sergeant smelled comfortably of his evening beer and his unlovely face was benevolent. His offerings were a crumpled cigarette and a hard army biscuit which he took squashed together from his pocket. Beside them in the prisoner's outstretched hand he placed two melting squares of dark Bourneville chocolate half in, half out of their silver wrapping. Better still, he splashed fresh water into the metal jug.

"Not a beanfeast maybe, Foxy, but the best I could muster from stock," he apologised, and the prisoner made long appreciative noises before he spoke his thanks.

"Home was never like this, sergeant."

"Betcher sweet life it weren't," the sergeant said. "Not that you'll see homeland for many a long day yet. Wot's in a bitta paper they want signing, tell me that?"

"I'll save the chocolate and the fag for later," the prisoner sidetracked. "I'm much obliged to you for your kindness, sergeant. I hope I'll be able to do something for you some day."

"Not if you don't sign their blasted paper, you won't. Two more of your blokes gone this morning."

"Gone home, you mean?"

"Gone to hell, the boss says, for not signing. Shot, mate." By this time the sergeant was sitting companionably on the boards beside him. "What's in it, Foxy … tell me that."

The prisoner was by now luxuriously biting noisy morsels off the hard biscuit which smelled of tobacco, and shaking his flaming head at the same time.

"I wish I could make you understand, sergeant. What I took part in wasn't just a brawl or a week-long riot as we heard some of your newspapers made out. It was a national movement, a revolution, to assert once again in arms the right of the Irish people to independence after seven hundred years of foreign misrule – yours, that is. Our leaders were professors and poets and idealists, men who knew we hadn't a chance militarily, although we didn't do too badly in the scrap to tell the truth of us. Now they are all dead, shot in revenge by your government which wants us to fight your war for you when we have no freedom ourselves. I'll make no apology and no promises to be of better behaviour in future just to be free to walk out of here when better men than me were glad and proud to give up their lives. 'Wrap the Green Flag Round Me, Boys,' was what we sang when Commandant Pearse ordered us to surrender to save innocent lives, and we marched through the ruins of O'Connell Street on the first lap to the transportation ships. Listen sergeant, listen and I'll tell you what we sang."

His big young voice filled the cell:

And though my body moulders, boys,
My spirit will be free,
And every comrade's honour, boys,
Will still be dear to me,
And in the thick and bloody fight
Nor let your courage lag
For I'll be there and hovering near
Around the dear old flag

"You've a nice bleeding voice," the sergeant said. But it's all a load of bullshit and codswallop. You're too bloody young to know, Foxy, that no country is worth dying for, and all dear old flags are the same if they're wrapped around your stinking corpse. Sign their bleeding paper and get out of here and live for your country like the rest of them."

"Living dishonourably ever after is not my cup of tea. I'd rather moulder as the song says."

"Honour – dishonour!" The sergeant's red face glowed more fiercely. "Words the quality thinks up over their mulled port wine and their big fat cigars. I was with those men lying for weeks in stinking trenches in Flanders until their feet rotted off them in one night's frost. I went off my rocker for a while meself after a shell burst beside me and I'm glad to say they invalided me out and set me watching blokes as refused to fight – bloody right they are too. Don't talk to me about honour and dishonour and the glory of bloody war. A fat lot of honour your poor bastard the general had when they set him up like an Aunt Sally at a fair. They tied him to a chair because his rotting foot wouldn't hold him up long enough to be shot dead. There's glory for ye!"

"That was General Connolly, I suppose?"

"Never could remember Paddies' names," the sergeant said. "Sweet dreams, Foxy."

"Could you get me a stub of pencil and some paper, sergeant? Anytime?"

"Maybe tomorrow, Foxy. Get to bye-byes now and pray Captain Allen don't do you for a troublesome bastard as he means to."

"Meaning?"

"Goodnight, Foxy, me lad. No more questions tonight."

The thought of the half-promised pen and paper, the fag and the precious chocolate, kept him going until the gas lamps bubbled their greenish light through the Judas hole. So long as he didn't smoke and didn't eat any more tonight, he had smoking and eating stored away for the taking. He drew the unlit cigarette luxuriously under his nostrils and he sniffed too at the homely smell of dark chocolate. On Saturdays his father would divide two bars of Bourneville among the six of them, and on Sundays his mother sometimes made them Fry's creamy cocoa instead of tea. She was harsh about money but she kept a good table, his mother.

Smelling that cocoa once again in his mind, he hid behind the door the crumpled cigarette and the square of chocolate. Then he had a long drink of fresh water and lay down on the planks once more, still smelling cocoa, determinedly putting the captain out of his mind. He couldn't pray, even, since the priests refused absolution to men going off with packed kit bags. He fell asleep at last with a steaming mug of cocoa warming his hands and the next minute the key rasped again in the door of his cell.

Only it wasn't the next minute, because a thin grey light showed through the bars of his window. Morning. And a soldier he had never seen before was standing with fixed bayonet ready to escort him somewhere. The soldier agreed to wait until the night's secretions had been deposited in the brown vessel in the corner and then he marched the prisoner before him along the silent cat cage. There was no sound yet from the other prisoners, no sound anywhere except their own echoing footsteps. They stopped before a small square room bright with several gaslights turned up full. Captain Allen looked spruce, combed and shaved except for his little moustache, and there was a smile in his handsome black eyes. He was sitting at a small table with pen, ink and paper before him.

"That will do, Parfitt. You may leave the prisoner until I call you."

"Very good, sir."

"You may wish me good morning, B323."

"Good morning, Captain Allen."

"Sir."

"Sir." The prisoner's shrug was hardly perceptible, but noted.

Captain Allen smiled, with the white well-brushed teeth. "I have something here I'd like you to identify, B323, if you would be so kind. How it came into my possession needn't concern you. Read it, if you please."

The prisoner was given into his astonished hands a broadsheet he knew very well. He had several copies of it at home. *Songs of Freedom* was the heading and three of the parodies had come from his own hand. He had had the satisfaction of hearing one of them sung in a fine big baritone voice by the postman doing his first rounds in Broadstone when he himself had been hurrying home from the night mail to bed. It was to this parody the officer's pink finger with its white half-moon was pointing now.

"Read it if you please, B323." The order was softly repeated and the prisoner took the broadsheet into his hand. The temptation was irresistible, and before he had consciously made a decision he heard his own voice ring out to the tune of 'Whack Fol the Diddle', managing to get through almost a complete stanza.

> *Joe Devlin sure he cannot grouse*
> *Whack fol the diddle lol the di-do-day*
> *For now he's "Leader" of the House*
> *Whack fol the diddle lol the di-do-day*
> *The party men stand overawed*
> *As Joe their slavery does applaud …*

The prisoner saw the pistol-blow coming but he went on singing until the stars burst in his head and his mouth seemed to be full of blood. When a glass of water was shakily offered him he took it and rinsed away into the proffered ashtray a broken side tooth from the lower jaw. When he looked up again at the officer's face it was ugly with bitterness and shame for what he had done.

"A semi-literate peasantry has ruined the planned progress of two parliamentary generations. We had Home Rule in the palm of our hand as soon as the war is over, but that wouldn't do the Paddywhacks – the brutish unthinking urban and rural peasantry, that hasn't changed for two hundred years."

"We?" the prisoner repeated, dabbing at his thickening lips with a handkerchief that had been given him, 'We?'"

"Do you think, my nearly-literate friend, that yours is the only sort of patriotic Irishman? Do you?"

The prisoner smiled and said once again that the leaders of this rebellion had been professors, poets, philosophers. He felt a sort of pity for the impassioned fellow Irishman with his handsome eyes and his pretty pink fingernails like a girl's. For a moment he thought conversation, even argument, might be possible. But the officer jabbed a hand bell on his desk, and violently ordered the sergeant to take the prisoner away.

They were recalled from half the length of the corridor and the familiar paper for signing was proffered, even with some gentleness. The prisoner shook his flaming head and the order to return him to his cell was given once again. He was no sooner there than a sergeant he had not seen before appeared at the door and ordered him to remove his clothes and boots. Dressed only in his coarse regulation drawers, the prisoner was marched through many corridors of the awakening prison to a wing that seemed miles away and silent as the other was busy.

The footsteps of the unknown sergeant rang out and returned in a hollow echo. The prisoner's bare feet made no sound. He was already very cold, and his lower jaw ached persistently, like his head. A distant clock chimed seven times as they came to a large door at the end of a stone passage. This was unlocked with some difficulty, the prisoner was ushered into a comparatively large square room with windows high up in the wall, and the door banged heavily behind the retreating guard.

It was so cold in the room that it might have been January instead of July. There was no comfort in the foggy grey light filtering through the windows and none for bare feet on the clean stone floor. But there was one good thing about it all the same. The room was big enough to run around and this the prisoner did, briskly from corner to corner, until, presumably, the guard would get back with a change of clothes. More felonious garments still? A hair shirt, perhaps, or shoes with spikes inside?

Once the blood got moving through his body again, he felt almost cheerful and quite equal to enduring the throb in his jaw. He found with his tongue the place where the broken tooth had been and he tasted blood again. But if all he got out of joining a revolution was a broken tooth, he was lucky. Even his feet didn't feel so cold now, but he kept running around on his toes anyway until he was exhausted. Then he set the bedboards on the trestles and lay down, a little exhilarated even as he waited for the guard to come down again with clothes and maybe even breakfast.

There was, however, no sound nearer than a distant clop of horseshoes on cobbled streets and he lay back listening as intently as the blood drumming in his ears would allow. A faraway dog gave a volley of short sharp barks and was silent again. A church bell sounded, and then a shrill prolonged whistle as a train pulled into

35

the faraway station. This was the homeliest sound of all and suddenly he was with the men on the footplate in the bustle of arrival, with them in the warm carriage-slamming world of another journey safely over, in the steaming splash of hot water and the rough comfort of the clean coarse towels, with them most of all as they sat gossiping over their steaming mugs of strong tea or sank their teeth into the crustiness of new bread. He closed his eyes and concentrated hard on hearing the first sounds that could mean his own approaching breakfast, but there were none, no familiar sound at all of an ordinary prison morning. Rather did the faint sounds that came to him now connect him with the unknown Cheshire town outside where ordinary people were beginning their day's work.

He thought he dozed for a while, but the cold woke him up again and he began again the pacing of his cell. His flesh was goosepimply now and his feet like ice again. He was evidently being punished for not signing the paper, or for cheekily singing "Election Results" for the captain with the silky voice, but why had his clothes been taken away? As his hunger raged on he thought lustfully of the two squares of chocolate and the squashed fag hidden in his cell, and he hoped if he never went back to claim them some other poor starving bastard would have the wit to find them. This gave him an idea and he searched his spacious new quarters with care.

Nothing. Not a crumb on the table, or caught in the back of the chair. Not even a break in the smooth white plaster of the walls, so eventually he set to behind the door where it might escape notice. His fingers were cold and it was hard to make the first break but he struck at the wall with the chair at last and was rewarded with a few flakes of plaster that tasted quite as good as the stuff in his own cell. There was no water to wash them down but he supposed they couldn't leave him forever without water. He started to run around his cell again until he realised that this made him thirstier so he stretched out on the bed again and lay with closed eyes willing his mind elsewhere, along the banks of the Royal Canal in March when swans nested among the greening weed, sitting for weeks on their ramshackle nests formed from rubbish people threw into the canal. As a child he used to watch for signs of the young ones, big grubby ungainly chicks that Hans Andersen wrote a story about. His thoughts idling among the reedy banks in sunshine, he was unprepared for the pistol shots, four of them that suddenly ripped into his consciousness.

He remembered the sergeant's words last night: "Two more of your blokes gone today ... to hell, the Captain says." The thought that he might be shot, that the execution yard might be here, this side of the jail, made him sit up sharply, forgetting that with his damaged jaw he should move slowly. Pain throbbed into his neck and up into the crown of his head and he sat for what seemed a long time on the edge of the boards, waiting for more shots. There were none. He thought perhaps his own execution might be the next, and that it would be heard by some other naked poor devil in a cell somewhere in the honeycomb.

He reminded himself that from the moment he packed his kit bag on that night of disputed mobilisation, he had known it might be for the last time. But he had known and agreed that he might be signing on for his own death long before, from the moment the small recruiting handbill caught his eye in the window of Shanahan's in Cuffe Street. That was March last year, nesting time along the Canal.

EMMET DIED TO FREE IRELAND.
WHAT ARE YOU DOING
TOWARDS THIS GLORIOUS OBJECT?
WHAT I CAN DO:
JOIN A VOLUNTEER COMPANY
WHICH WILL TRAIN YOU
TO BEAR ARMS IN IRELAND'S CAUSE.

They had trained him to bear arms in Ireland's cause every Friday night between eight and ten o'clock in St Joseph's Hall, and they had taught him to jump and vault properly which might be useful to an actor if he ever made the full-time grade, and they had taught him signalling and first-aid and musketry. He had been commended for his progress and he had shown up well on rainy weekend manoeuvres in the Dublin mountains. Only that he sometimes came to meetings in his fireman's uniform straight off the job, he thought he might have been made an officer, but it didn't worry him. He accepted that the officers always wore a collar and tie and had neatly kept hands that seldom lifted anything heavier than a pen. Born himself to hard manual work and the necessity to conduct his own education if he wanted that luxury, he admired their patiently acquired toughness in the field, the way they ignored blistered hands and feet and cold and exposure which to him were normal. He remembered most of all the bravery of Commandant Daly during the fight and the way his men always came first, first for food, first for rest.

He remembered the day he had come closest to his commanding officer after the week's fiercest battle when they found the six mown-down British Tommies in a heap together near the head of Church Street, like boys who had tumbled over in a game. He knew that Ned Daly and himself were united in not seeing them any more as the ancient enemy but as sons and brothers who would go home no more and who hadn't even the glory of dying out on the Western Front. Their families and friends would see this as death in a brawl in Ireland, stupid, ignoble, soon to be forgotten like other brawls. Death by accident almost. A pity but not a glory, nothing to boast of as their death in Flanders would have been. Yet the fact of their death was the same. Their lives were over, and like himself they were not yet twenty. Flies were feasting on the open face of one of them, and Commandant Daly covered it with the boy's fallen cap.

The prisoner suddenly remembered that Ned Daly, like Pearse and Connolly, must be dead now, who had been gentle with death. He made the sign of the cross and tried again to pray, but then he remembered hearing that some priests had even refused absolution to dying Volunteers. These cowardly men of God were worse than the Carthaginians in whose power he was now. Carthaginians Mitchel had called them (as he had called the Catholic church "the enemy of Irish freedom") even although they allowed him books and the materials to write his Journal. Pen and ink actually to write the words that now came unbidden back to him – had he ever learned them, as he'd learned Michael's lines or did they stay imprinted on his mind for ever from the moment he read them?

"We must openly glorify arms until young Irishmen burn to handle them and try their temper; and this we must do in defiance of the "law" – deny that it is law; deny that there is any power in the London parliament to make laws for us and declare that as a just God ruleth in the earth we shall obey such laws no longer."

He shouted the words out loud, jumped up from the planks and beat with his fist on the door and shouted them again. There were no Carthaginians around to hear but that couldn't be helped. At the top of his voice he shouted again what Mitchel had shouted to his Journal, that he would "hurl the fires of Hell at the British Empire" before he signed a paper implicitly apologising for what he had done and promising to be of good behaviour in future. In future? What future?

His hands fallen by his sides, he realised for the first time the significance of the large, almost comfortable cell and the remote empty wing. This was where they sent men to be away from the rest of the prisoners at the end. This was the condemned cell and these were his last hours. It was all nonsense what he had heard about the fags and the good food you got before they shot you. He had been jailed without trial and now he would be dispatched without food and worst of all without the stub of a pencil to make his farewells or write his testament. The fellow Irishman with the beautiful hands had taken sophisticated revenge for the gross impertinence of a prisoner's behaviour. If it be so, Mitchel used to say, be it so. No crumpled letter of farewell to his family or comrades, no scribbled word of thanks to Frances Montgomery of some place near the Bishop's Palace. All around her hat she might even wear a tricoloured ribbon-o … If only she knew. If she came to see him again what would they tell her? Would word be sent to his mother? Shot while trying to escape? That was sufficient excuse, he believed.

He looked up at the small high window and saw that it was filling with honey light brimming through the bars. With his back against the cold cell door he listened deliberately to the morning and thought he could distinguish the rattle of milk carts and again the distant clop of hooves on cobblestones. The town clock struck and he counted the strokes. Seven. Seven o'clock of a July morning, maybe the last morning of his life. If he were sure he could look it in the face and not be afraid. "For from the graves of patriot men and women spring living nations," Commandant Pearse had said over the grave of the old Fenian. Pearse and all his comrade leaders were lying in such graves now, all together in quicklime maybe, for all he knew.

It didn't perhaps matter where one died, or how solitary the grave. What mattered was not being afraid, and in humility making the sacrifice of what poor future one believed one had. He didn't think he was afraid. Starved and still cold he was, despite the warm honey-coloured light, but not afraid. "Be my prison where it will, I suppose there is a heaven above that place," Mitchel had

41

said, and he too supposed there was. But if he had the choice between the slim books of the New Testament and the thumb-tattered *Jail Journal* he kept beside his bed at home, he knew which he would choose. He was what the books he had read and the lines that had been a trumpet call had made him. All he had to offer was his own life, such as it was. He'd like (who wouldn't?) to have fallen with his leaders, to have gone out in a blaze during Commandant Daly's great fight.

He would like (and the wish he knew was an arrogant wish) to have added his life physically to theirs though he wasn't a leader and had only followed in a light-hearted, even frivolous way. And so his death would be like the deaths of the poor English bastards in North King Street, an afterthought, a sort of accident, not really related to the sum total of the sacrifice. But no matter. He knew he wasn't afraid and that was something. It could be that when the town clock struck eight he would be standing blindfold in the sunny yard, wearing some sort of clothes, he hoped, and not, positively not, afraid to die. He might be afraid of a hanging death, but he had heard the shots off and on during the summer that meant somewhere men had died. He supposed shooting was quicker and cheaper than hanging and that was why Irish prisoners were shot when necessary rather than as the concession to them of a soldier's death. No green flag after all would be wrapped around him, but to hell with that. The worst he had to put up with until eight o'clock was the itch to write, anything, even his name.

Bent on one knee he tried to scratch it behind the door with his fingernail but it wasn't very successful. If they brought him even a bowl of gruel he knew he could scratch something with his spoon, but they wouldn't feed him now. Breakfast was long over. And what need had a man of breakfast when his life had dwindled to one hour from now?

But one hour from then he was incredulously listening to the town clock striking eight, pleasant mellow notes in the summer air. There were no other sounds, no scrape of boots or clatter of bayonets as an armed guard came to conduct him into the yard. No sounds of any kind except the distant hum of the town that was no more than the purring of a giant cat unless one deliberately listened for and distinguished one small sound or another. He did that for a long time later on as he grew warmer with the day outside and so far beyond the edges of hunger that he didn't feel it any more. He could still offer no prayers but he spoke aloud James Clarence Mangan, and Emmet's speech from the dock, and some of Tom Moore, and "The Night Before Larry Was Stretched", and he tried to continue with a comic parody he was making to the air of "The Harp and Lion".

> *Says Dan when I met him one day*
> *A word with you I'd like to say –*
> *Kate's hand in love you'll ne'er attain*
> *Except you give up this Sinn Fein*
> *Sore heads and cranks the "Freeman" calls you*
> *Even that does not …*

Does not what? Does not appal you? Doesn't rhyme but it will do for the moment. His voice rang out and echoed and died away but he kept up the pastime. It wasn't a very good parody but then he'd noticed that it wasn't the very good ones people took up. Frequently the contrary. He had three more verses (knowing how much better they would be if only he had paper and a stub of pencil) when he noticed the light was fading and somehow the day had worn away.

He was pattering around the stone floor to ease his cramped limbs again when he heard the first sounds (for how many hours?) in this wing. A laugh and the scrape of boots and a bayonet jingle. He leaped at the door and battered on it with his fists, shouting at the top of his voice for somebody to come and tell him why the hell he was being starved to death and on whose orders. The footsteps came nearer and in the greenish gaslight through the opened spyhole he saw two white-faced Tommies who gaped at him in apparent terror and ran away.

He set up an even louder clamour at the door, yelling at the top of his healthy lungs, and at last he heard the sound of boots again on the landing. Several pairs: he could not imagine why so many should be required to attend to one naked prisoner. A key rasped in the lock and the door swung open. The original pair of Tommies were standing as far back as they could get, against the opposite wall. An officer among the group asked him who he was, and raised small arched eyebrows when he got the answer,

"Irish prisoner."

"Why are you in this cell?"

The prisoner lost his head then and raved with his dry damaged mouth that made his voice sound to him like rattling peas in a box. About how he found it a pleasant place to spend a summer's day, and how much better it would be if they hadn't taken his clothes away and if he had been given the usual generous rations or even allowed water. About the fires of hell and the Empire and what Captain Allen could do with his lousy paper and what Mitchel thought of British justice and a lot more.

The small neat officer remained superior and impassive. "I understand how you feel, young man. I'll have this strange matter investigated. Return this prisoner to his block, men, and see that his clothes are returned and that he is fed a good meal immediately."

"Yes, sir."

"And you, Brown, ask Captain Allen to be good enough to come to my quarters."

"Very good, sir."

Nothing was ever the same again. The letters from his family which were put all together with another letter into his hand were as good to get as that first meal of his new life. Next day they gave him a thick writing pad, a couple of N pens and a bottle of Stephen's ink. The second letter he wrote, after the one home, was to Frances Montgomery.

> *The feel of a pen between my fingers again is even better than I knew it would be, and it's a pleasure to be able to thank you at last for your letter and for coming to see me. The contents of the parcel were delicious and most welcome but next time it will be enough just to see you. You say your eldest sister Harriet will come too when she is*

*over here – does she write poetry like you? And
will she be as slow to show it to a poor devil who
has his tongue hanging out for culture just now?
I have asked for books, however, and I'm told my
request will be forwarded to the right quarter "in
due course". When I see you again I have a tale
to tell will curdle your young blood ...*

Already he saw himself a creature of legend, Othello to
the golden girl who might pity him for dangers he had
passed.

The Sisters

Going by tram to the other side of the city was part of the treat. The child was usually quick enough to escape up the stairs when they got on at the Pillar and take her seat out in the front where you were always blown by the breeze and close to the exciting flashes of the wires overhead. Her mother, laughing though with exasperation, would follow her up the stairs and sit just inside the upper compartment with the door closed against the breeze but with a good view of all her daughter might be doing. When it rained, Emily would be called in, but she would always shout that it was only a few drops and would soon be over. Her mother couldn't hear her through the glass door but that didn't matter. If the rain were persistent Emily would be hauled in protesting that she would be sick inside, which she always pretended to be and sometimes was. Unless in the case of a positive downpour she usually had her way. She felt like a queen riding in a high carriage, ruler of everything spread beneath her: small people with short scurrying legs, men under the crowns of soft hats which appeared to be perched on faceless necks, carthorses rattling over the cobbles, babies in prams small as the one Emily pushed into the hall of her doll's house.

There were trees too and green lawns passing the railings to your left before you swung right at Elvery's where the elephant was. You could look into the elephant's small eyes which were about level with your own and feel at times that a stretched out hand could touch the tassels of his headgear. But stretching out your hand on the outside of the tram was strictly forbidden. There were fearful stories of electrocuted arms and hands knocked off as you passed lamp posts and if you broke the rules so flagrantly you could be brought in for good and angrily pinned to the seat inside.

There was a big green shop past Elvery's and it sold garden swings and lawnmowers and little white tables for having tea in the garden. That was what they sometimes had at Aunt Harry's. You went up a big flight of stone steps to Harry's hall door and so you had to go down a short flight of steps in the back hall and down more stone steps outside the back door to get into the garden. It was bigger than any other garden Emily knew, even her grandfather's, and it had pink brick walls and apple trees and a sundial but it had no swing. When she was let out there straight away she knew her mother and her aunt were going to talk about money. Once over tea in the garden Aunt Harry took her mother's hand before giving her a teacup and stared hard at the wedding ring. That was what Emily thought, anyway, but it wasn't at the wedding ring.

"So it's gone again?" Harry said, and her mother laughed uneasily.

"I'll probably be getting it out again at the end of the month when there should be some overtime."

"What poor mother would have thought I daren't imagine. God spared her the knowledge of the mistake you made."

This mistake was a frequent subject for comment by Harry. It had something to do with the size of the house they lived in and the small brother or sister that Emily had been told would be sharing her bedroom soon. Aunt Harry had a lot of dolls but no children in her house. It was bigger than any house Emily had ever been in. If her aunt offered to let her play with dolls in the bedroom she knew she must first say no, because her mother always signalled to her with her eyes. If she stayed, Aunt Harry often made jokes and fetched a big beach ball when tea was over, but if Emily went to play with the dolls she would see her mother's and aunt's heads wagging in disagreement when she looked down out of the big bedroom window beyond the laburnum tree.

"Like to play with the dolls, today, Emily love?"

"No thanks – unless I could bring the dolls down to the garden."

"You know you can't do that, Emily. Fetch down the ball if you like from the hall chest."

"All right."

"Say 'thank you,' Emily." That was her mother.

"All right, thank you."

Sometimes even when she had been away for a short time because she ran all the way back, her mother would be blowing her nose or giggling uneasily when Emily came back.

"There is no need to discuss it any further. You know my views on the subject of borrowing," Aunt Harry might be saying.

One day in winter after tea by the fire in the big front room, Emily's mother had shown signs of holding her own. "I can easily check when I go home but I do think these are my teaspoons. Yours had no shell edging like these ones, Harry."

"Nonsense, dear."

"The ones mother gave you were the silver apostle spoons, I distinctly remember. The last time I used my silver spoons was at Christmas time when you and Richard came over on Stephen's night. You washed up for me, remember?"

"Very well, dear, I did take the spoons but only for safe keeping, knowing your careless ways. The next time it might be the spoons as well and where would you get the interest on both I should like to know? Of course you may have them back when things improve for dear Bartholomew if they ever do."

"I may have them back if things improve!" Now to Emily's delight her mother was laughing, or rather giggling with the back of her hand against her mouth. "Oh, Harry, you'll be the death of me yet!"

"You know I'm usually right, Fanny dear. You won't be tempted to do anything foolish if poor Mother's silver teaspoons aren't under your hand."

"Perhaps you're right. Would you like to take Mother's copper coal scuttle as well and the big blue dinner service and the Laughing Cavalier?"

"Those things are not so easily disposed of. Have another scone, Fanny dear."

That evening when Uncle Richard came in with his brief case from the office, he drank a cup of tea quickly and then took Emily for a walk although it was so cold. He buttoned up her gaiters himself and wound a big scarf twice around her neck. They went down the Lansdowne Road to the Dodder.

"Why does Aunt Harry take the silver spoons away when she comes to our house, Uncle?"

"God bless my soul – what an idea, Emily! Where did you get this fancy from? Look at the robin over there and how he isn't afraid."

"He can't see us."

"Oh yes he can. They can see sideways. The eyes are at the side of their head, do you see?"

"Why does Aunt Harry sometimes make Mother cry? She never cries at home."

"Don't walk too near the edge and I'll tell you a story. Once upon a time there were two princesses." The river was noisy running over the stones. In summer you could see pinkeens but never in the winter. "When the little princesses were children they played together and never quarrelled but when they grew up their mother died and the elder princess had to help the king to rule and keep everything going just as ever and then the sisters often quarrelled and the younger even hated the elder at times. But the people in the land were still happy because it was still ruled as well as when the queen was alive. Then the king died and the younger sister married the young prince they both loved but the elder sister who was queen now had to make do with an older prince who had a lot of money and wasn't very handsome. So they quarrelled more than ever whenever they met but they loved each other all the same."

"What else?"

"Nothing else. That's the story. It's not very new and in fact it's as old as the hills – and if you don't like it you can always make up a better one yourself."

"Daddy's stories are always more exciting. And funnier." She knew she was being very rude but Richard didn't seem to mind.

"Does he tell you a story every night in bed?"

"Not every night. Not a story every night. Sometimes he tells me to close my eyes and we get on a train called the Slumberland Express. You can hear the steam getting up and the doors of the carriages rattling and children talking to one another and then the carriage doors banging and the guard blowing his whistle. And the train goes slowly at first then faster and faster and faster …"

"And he makes all the noises himself?"

"When the train is really going fast you're asleep so you don't know. If I wanted to get off I couldn't. The next time I see him is shaving next morning. He puts soap on my face too. Then he goes off to work in the gas company. Where do you work?"

"In an office."

"Is it your own office or somebody else's office?"

"My own office. Do you know what that is down there?"

"A heap of old newspapers and sticks and ice-cream packets and somebody's old shirt."

"Wrong. It's a swan's nest. Next week or so you might see a swan sitting on it.'

"Can we come next week?"

"If Aunt Harry invites you, yes, and we'll go for a walk again, just the two of us."

"Couldn't you invite me?"

"Yes, but I gave up doing that sort of thing years ago. It usually didn't work out, you see."

The river path ended in a scatter of little houses with hens picking around them and up at the bridge the trams were turning round to go back into town with a lot of electric flashes against a lemon sky. When they got to the kiosk at the top of Pembroke Road he bought the Evening Mail final for himself and butterscotch for her in a white packet with C & B in gold along the edge, and the steps up to the house were steeper than when she arrived with her mother and one of them grazed her knee but it didn't hurt much.

After supper Richard took a bottle out of the sideboard and poured some for everybody but Aunt Harry tipped a little out of one glass and into Richard's before handing it to Emily's mother. Emily's glass had only a little port wine in the bottom and was filled up with warm water.

"Now Fanny, your health," Richard smiled. "And yours, Emmy." The fire scorched her legs but the orange satin cushion with the silk tassels cooled them again.

"Have you been thinking over what we were talking about Fanny?" Aunt Harry said, taking her port in tiny sips. Her smile was tight.

"Oh yes."

"And what do you think, dear? Is it not a good idea, all things considered? I'm sure dear Bartholomew wouldn't stand in the way of a good sensible plan."

"Yes, I'm afraid he would. He doesn't like the idea at all, you see."

Emily knew it was one of those occasions when

it was useless to ask questions, so she took a piece of butterscotch, carefully unwrapping it and tossing the rolled paper ball in the fire where it sizzled because it was greased paper.

"Won't you offer your packet around, Emily?" That was her mother. Apologising for having forgotten, Emily did that. They all thanked her.

"And why on earth would Bartholomew not think it a good idea seeing the way things are with no hope of improvement, rather the reverse?"

"He plans to organise a branch of the Workers' Union of Ireland and campaign for better wages and stability, he says. The workers just need to be organised, you see."

"I see that Bartholomew will end up without any job at all, like the last time he went to war. Typical of him to stir up trouble again instead of buckling down and getting all the overtime they can give him."

"He says they should be paid higher rates for overtime, not the same."

"He doesn't know his own luck in these hard times. Nothing will ever be the same again after '29. Doesn't he know that?"

"Why don't you discuss it with Mull himself?" It was clear now that Emily's mother was angry.

"I think," said Richard, "we should all drink up and even have a little more. Even get a bit tiddly. We'll talk about all this another time, eh, Harry?"

"No time like the present, especially when time is so short. Did you make everything quite clear to Bartholomew? That we would be responsible for education, clothing and all other expenses?"

"Yes, I did," Emily's mother said. "It's a generous offer. But you see we don't ..."

"You'll see E-M-I-L-Y very often, dear – it isn't as though we lived at the other end of the country. You will come to us and we will go over to you especially when the baby is too small to travel. Have no doubt about it, Fanny, it's the ideal solution in your situation. The child is worth the best money can buy and you should know where money is shortest, just now and for a long time to come I'm afraid. Be sensible and unselfish like a dear good girl. I'm sure it's what poor Mother would have suggested if God had spared her."

"Mother didn't part with any single one of eight children and I'm not going to either, so there!" Emily's mother blazed out at last and then immediately burst into tears. Richard fussed around her and Emily stood with one hand on her mother's knee. "I think I'd like to go home," she said.

"She'll be able to have music lessons, riding ..."

"We are s-s-saving up to buy a piano."

"Your lawful debts must be disposed of first, I should imagine. She'll even be able to go to the university. Think of the future, Fanny."

"That's enough, Harriet. You've said enough for one day. Let it be now." That was Richard, always the peacemaker.

"I want to go home, please."

"Very well, I've got something for you before you go, Emmy." When Harry called her Emmy she always wanted something. "Something you've always wanted, Emmy. Come till I show you, there's a little love."

55

Her mother signalled to her to go, and the something was apparently in Harriet's bedroom. The place smelled of mothballs and eau de cologne and it was icy cold after the fire, but because of red chenille curtains and a red lampshade it looked warm. Harriet lifted down one of the rag dolls pinned to the red silk bell-pulls beside her mantelpiece. Turkey legs.

"Now love, that's for you to take home and keep."

"No, thank you, that's the one with turkey legs."

"Turkey legs?"

"They're sort of dead and bare like a turkey hanging up in the butcher's. I don't like them. Thank you very much but I don't want to take the doll home."

"She was here before," Harry said, sighing, when the went back to the drawing room. "I don't know who she takes after but she was here before. Have a bar of Fry's cream chocolate then, Emmy, to eat on the tram." Chocolate was stored in the oak and silver biscuit barrel on the sideboard.

"Thank you very much, Aunt Harry."

Harriet waved to them from the top of the steps and Uncle Richard saw them to the tram. A cold wind whipped around the kiosk which was dark and closed up now. There were blue stars above the tram lines.

"Don't mind Harry," Richard was saying, squeezing his sister-in-law's arm. "You know the way she's always wanting to manage everything. You see she's so good at it, better than the rest of us put together. But if I had a whole houseful of children I wouldn't part with one either. I understand your attitude completely, Francoise."

He had volunteered for France during the war and liked to remind people, her mother had told Emily, that he had learned to speak a little French. A tram came swaying along from Blackrock and he put half a crown into Emily's pocket.

"Don't be any more reckless than I'd be myself, Emily," he smiled. Half a crown was unimaginable wealth.

"Thank you very much, Uncle Richard." She kissed his cheek when he laid it against hers. It was thin and cold and smelled of shaving soap.

"Chin up, my love, and if you can't be good, be careful," he said jauntily to Emily's mother as he handed her onto the boarding platform. He swung Emily up beside her and though she was too big for that sort of thing she didn't mind. Beside her on the platform was an advertisement which said LOBO, delicious sweets and chocolates, 9 Lower Baggot Street. Her mother hauled her firmly into the lower compartment.

"Can't we go up, can't we, to see the lights?"

"It's too cold up there at night-time. Wave to Uncle Richard, there's a good girl."

They waved to Uncle Richard until he was a small speck surrounded by a blowing white scarf and he waved to them. Her mother held her tightly clasped as though she were a baby again. The tram swayed and rattled and Emily closed her eyes trying to remember what the street lamps were like when you were looking down on them from the top of the tram. At night you had a feeling of flying with shops and houses and people far below under the wavering lamplight. It was best of all when the streets were wet with rain and the lights were doubled, glimmering back up at you from the pavements. The swaying movement of the tram reminded her suddenly of the Slumberland Express and she never knew whether her father actually met them at the tram stop or whether she dreamed he did.

Humane Vitae

After rain, the washed blue sky glittered above the choppy sea, but the east wind was cold. "See," the man in the sheepskin coat said smugly, "I brought that bit of sun with me." Clichés were so seldom used as opening gambits that the wife glanced sharply at him before smiling.

"I could show you the Mass rock I wrote to you about," she said with some diffidence, at last. "It's better in the very late evening, just before sunset, but it may be raining by then."

"Almost certainly. So show me. Not more than seven miles there and back."

"It's much less, honestly. Michael and I did it a few nights ago before his bedtime. Mrs O'Friel puts the others to bed for me whenever I want to go out."

"Nice Mrs O'Friel. I liked her immediately."

Once again the wife glanced up, surprised and pleased, as she tried to measure her quick strides to his slow ones over the rocky fields behind the house. "She was delighted when she heard you were coming up for the last week – you wouldn't believe the fuss there was the last few days. She wanted to know would I like to change my room when the Flynns went because the wardrobe was bigger and you could see the headland from that window – it's called Reenamara, by the way. Look, over there."

"Oh, yes."

"It's where you get the best lobsters. Wee Tommy fishes them out from under the rocks with a stick which has a hook on the end of it."

"You've seen this?"

"Yes. The boys and I went on a lobster hunt with the O'Friels last week. The Flynns and some others came too. You must come with us one day next week."

"Who's Wee Tommy while he's at home or abroad?"

"He's Mr O'Friel. But nobody calls him anything except Wee Tommy – he's so small that his son Hugh could carry him for seven miles on his back without even noticing the difference."

"Hugh does this often?"

"Don't be silly!" The wife, giggling, skipped ahead at last at her own pace, jumping from one reedy tussock of grass to another over the marshy pale green patches which at dusk could be treacherous. She went on skipping until she reached the first grey slabs of rock, and then she sat down and lifted her face to the sun, eyes closed, leaning back on the palms of her hands, smiling.

Just before the man reached her, he became aware that she was watching his slow progress through smiling slitted eyes, and he stumbled on one of the tussocks, misjudged the jump to the next one, and ended up cursing on the pale boggy moss, up to the tops of his socks in water. Her laugh died quickly when she saw his angry face, but he was beside her laughing at himself in a few moments.

"This was never my country," he intoned, "I was not born nor bred nor reared here and it will not have me alive nor dead. But it may well be the end of me!"

She laughed and went on laughing. "Take off your socks," she said, "and I'll hang them out of my belt to dry in the wind." She was wearing blue denims with a sort of leather scout's belt which had loops made for carrying various objects.

"They'll dry just as quickly on me, and probably much quicker," the man said.

"Wee Tommy wouldn't agree with you about ignoring wet feet. You know what he does? Before he steps out into the shallow pools at low tide he takes off his socks and puts them in his pocket. Then he rolls up his trouser legs and puts his boots back on again."

"You mean wellingtons?"

"I mean ordinary black leather boots. And he steps out into the pool in those so that they're sopping wet by the time he's finished."

"Don't tell me. Then he takes them off and puts on his dry socks. Then he puts his boots back on, and before he's gone ten paces his socks are as wet as the boots! He could have saved himself a lot of trouble by just stepping out in the first place."

"You're wrong. The dry socks stay dry, he says, and the boots have dried out by the time he gets home."

"Obstinate, self-deceiving peasants!" the man exploded, but good-humouredly, and he took her hand to pull her to her feet. He kept the hand in a tight grip as they walked along, as easily as though on a road because here the rocks were in flat slab formations. Small pink flowers like candytuft grew in the crevices and bent double in the sea wind. The sea itself had temporarily disappeared, though they could hear its roaring in the caves underneath.

"How was it at home when you left this morning?" the wife asked.

"All right. Mrs Cuffe says to tell you the dogs were so lonely for you that they've begun to be friendly with her and they even eat the tinned stuff occasionally."

"Poor dogs. What about you?"

"OK. I've been messing with the sun place and you may even like it."

"What have you done?"

"Wait and see. And I let the grandchildren staying next door strip the raspberries, and then I did over the paths with sodium chlorate. Oh, and Mrs Cuffe took home some windfalls to make apple jelly."

"Did Joan ask you over to a meal as she said?"

"She did, but I managed to get out of it."

"Michael!"

"I was perfectly tactful, don't worry."

"Wait till you taste a lobster that's been only out of the tide half an hour! After weeks of basic eating you're going to enjoy this week, I can tell you. We'll probably go out with Wee Tommy again – let's see, this is Saturday. Tuesday the tide should be right again for lobsters. I'll bet he'll be going on Tuesday and we can all go with him."

"You've forgotten I don't particularly like the beasts."

"Wait till you taste one that's been crawling around

the kitchen floor until the moment it's put into the boiling water!"

Cormorants screamed around their heads as they climbed the last barbed-wire fence stubbornly fixed to the bare rock. "Who," the man wanted to know, "but these land-hungry famine relicts would bother to fix a boundary to such a barrenness? Who would be likely to dispute ownership with them except these gulls?"

"If it were mine I'd do exactly the same," the wife said. "Look, this is the last stretch. Do you see where the rocks form a sort of semi-circle, like half a Greek stage? Well, that's Carraig-an-Aifrinn. It's just at the innermost point."

"Let's say we've seen it, then. Look at those clouds making straight for us." Rain clouds had clotted together beyond the next headland and were blowing lightly as the white cumulus across the dwindling stretch of the blue sky.

"It will just about catch us, if it does rain, when we've arrived at the rick and there we have shelter."

She broke away as she had done earlier and ran, beckoning him, across the bright granite, her ridged shoes gripping fast even when she leaped across the now frequent gashes in the rock face through which the sea spumed below. The man shrugged and buttoned his sheepskin higher, then followed in the same direction, though not in her footsteps. When he chose he could stride faster than she and this he did, avoiding most of the jumps by taking the long way around them, and arriving at the fan-like circle of rocks only a little after she did and only a little more breathless.

"See if you can find it," she invited, elbows leaning on a low table of rock that was not a dolmen but looked very similar. The man fancied he could actually feel the cold stone against her breasts; she could never be taught to wear enough clothes.

"You're irreverently leaning on it, of course."

"Wrong. I wouldn't." She was smiling.

The man shrugged and buttoned his collar up against the first blown drops of rain. Then he quickly stepped around her side of the rock, pulled a blue scarf out of her pocket and tied it under her chin.

"What's wrong with you is you are not safe to let out," he said, but now he was smiling. "Look, while you propose this cute game of hide-and-seek those dirty black clouds are about to disgorge their whole load on top of us." Still smiling, the wife shook off her scarf and beckoned him. He followed, into the broken circle of rocks, some of which dripped as though the sea had somehow forced entry from below and bled through them. But when she stopped abruptly and stepped behind a mound of small rocks – like the cairn on a mountain summit – it was suddenly dry, and the limestone altar was unmistakable though much smaller than the exposed table he had seen at first. Up behind it the rock face with its savage fissures soared a hundred feet into the air so that one thought of a Gothic cathedral until one came face to face with the sky, with the one triangle of blue that remained.

"Look!" the wife said, and put a small heap of coins into his hand. He had not noticed that the altar was littered with these, sixpenny pieces and shillings of worn silver, halfpence and pence and (surely?) a couple of half-sovereigns. These were what she had put into his hand and he turned them over curiously.

"Can't understand how somebody hasn't knocked them off." he said. "How did they escape?"

"Who would take them? It's a holy place."

When he turned from replacing the gold coins she was on her knees, fair head bent, but she got up almost immediately when a rainy bitter gust of wind practically took their breath away.

"I know where to go," she said, and he followed her a few yards away into a shallow cave, invisible from where they had been standing. Inside, it was dry, with a floor of small pebbles and the shells of sea-snails which, some time, might have been carried there by high tides. Pleased, he took off his sheepskin and spread it inside out on the pebbles. Suddenly he was reminded of their courtship. When she plumped down, giggling at the perfection of the shelter she had provided, he was instantly beside her, bulky and warm, breathing very fast, amorous suddenly as was his way, joking about the ghosts of the decent Mass-going peasants that were this very minute about to be startled.

The wife's quick initial response was suddenly checked, and she broke from him to sit suddenly back on her heels, cold hands cupping her knees. She saw the astonishment in his eyes and her voice did not quite register the levity she had intended.

"Perhaps we'd better make a date for same time, same place on Monday. It ought to have been OK today, but I was late, and it isn't. Unless you want twins or something by this time next year."

"Oh God, no!" At home he'd even checked the marked calendar on the inside of his wardrobe. But this was a calendar you could never quite rely on. Yet he had relied on it for the whole length of that journey. Two hundred miles had never seemed so short.

"You're not any sorrier than I am," she complained, turning away to dig into the small pebbles with her fingers.

"Sorry, yes, but you'll go on waiting for a celibate churchman in Mother Rome to change his mind again, won't you? How long is it going to take him to realise that though he may have spoken, the people of God have long since passed out of earshot?"

"I haven't and he isn't just a celibate churchman. He's the Pope."

"You haven't. And he's the Pope. And he has the right to tell you when your marriage vows made before God may be honoured and when not."

"Yes, he has the right," the wife said, on the note of stubborn finality that goes with old arguments. She was still playing with a handful of the small pebbles as he got angrily to his feet and stamped over to the mouth of the cave. For several minutes he stared out into the driving rain. Once she thought he was going to make off into it, but he came back shaking himself like a dog with something like calm restored to his face.

"Don't imagine I came all the way up here to go into all that again," he said.

"Monday's not really so far away," the wife placated, and he opened his mouth to reply but quickly changed his mind.

He went on to another tack. "Trouble with you is you never see beyond these desolate rainy wastes. Look at us! Huddled on a summer's day in a damp cave on the edge of the Atlantic with the rain and the furious sea thundering all around us and not even sex to keep us warm, and you think we should be happy."

"I am. And the floor of the cave is bone dry – feel!"

"Out there are sun and civilisations the sun nurtured – do you think the culture of Greece could have happened at all in a climate like this?"

"You can hardly call this place uncivilised all the same. Think of the imagination that saw this as the perfect natural place of worship that it is – and closely hidden as it had to be."

"Think of them," the man said, "struggling in their famine tatters across the rocks with the rain beating down on them, spouting their barbaric language at one another, with their fists clenched tight over the halfpence they wouldn't have been welcomed without."

"Not true. The celebrant of a Penal Mass risked death every time he celebrated it, remember. If he had to live on the halfpence of the poor, that was hardly his fault. They gave freely."

"What puzzles me is why they continued to give when the whole show was over. What's the meaning of these coins, most of which are no more than a century old. Don't tell me any priest couldn't bear to take the pence of the poor."

"It puzzles me too. I think maybe the money was offered up perhaps in gratitude for Emancipation or something."

"Offered to God? Money? You see, your own particular form of superstitious lunacy. Like the Thanksgiving notices you see only in Irish newspapers. 'Grateful thanks to St Anthony for great favour received.' Is the Irish Independent delivered by carrier pigeon to the celestial gates at ten o'clock sharp every morning? Or does St Anthony come down for a free read of the files every so often to find out who are the lousers who won't even bother to thank him?"

Now the wife was laughing too, but she stopped soon. "I'm taking you to meet Paid Loin tonight in O'Donnell's pub,' she said. "He'll tell you more than I can about this place – which, by the way, is haunted."

"We are not going to listen to a sean duine liath giving out old guff over his booze tonight?"

"Of course we are. It's great fun, and I promise you'll like him. Aren't you curious to know about who haunts Carraig-an-Aifrinn? That I do know."

"It's haunted by a pair of drunken tailors who dropped three halfpence through a slit in the rock on the way to Mass one rainy morning after Samhain. They've never given up hope of finding the money. So every night when the moon is full … "

"Keep quiet and listen. Two men and a pregnant woman came over in a curragh from the island one Sunday morning. Can you imagine landing a curragh on those rocks down there even in good weather? It seems the woman's brother was capable of handling a curragh anywhere along this coast and her husband was nearly as good. But a storm blew up suddenly – it was October – and they were drowned trying to land. They were seen in

68

broad daylight on the edge of the crowd at Mass a short time afterwards and they still haunt these rocks."

"Very nice. Pregnant with her thirteenth child no doubt. Now come on before we hear them caterwauling – God knows, it's dark enough, though the rain seems to have stopped." He pulled her to her feet, kissed her lightly by way of peace offering, and buttoned himself back into his sheepskin. They strolled, arm in arm, back along the wet roads of rock.

"Look,' said the wife, "I wouldn't doubt him. Will you look at Michael coming out to find us?"

The ten-year-old in an Aran gansy was bounding like a goat towards them over the rocks, whooping a war cry in case they hadn't seen him. He arrived breathless but articulate. "The others are furious, Daddy, that you got away without them. I guessed where Mummy had taken you so I thought – thought I'd just meet you on the way back." He grinned, his freckled face sheepish.

"Well timed, Michael," the father applauded.

"Know what?" the boy said in his mother's ear. "Hugh's just brought in a huge salmon for Daddy's supper."

"You don't mean it?"

"Sure. And Daddy, Hugh says will you come out fishing with us in the boat on Monday?"

"I couldn't bear the cold in my aged bones."

"But Daddy, he has oilskins for us, and I was too hot out in the boat last week – even in the rain."

"Look at those other scoundrels coming out after you," the man said abruptly, and when they waved the four remote figures in blue shorts scrambled like crabs over the rocks, uttering faint aggrieved shouts as they came.

Up in the ghost village of Kilcreeshla there were hardly any lights. The green road that led to another village (now totally deserted) was invisible to all but those who knew it was there. Kilcreeshla itself had only four school-going children and as many as forty old people, so most of the stone cottages which were not abandoned were asleep early and showed no lights. Two houses built together at right angles to the road were bright, however, and bicycles leaned against the gable end. A few visitors' cars were parked together in the open flagged yard where hens picked during the daytime. When the door opened, a blast of warm talk and firelight escaped into the night air, but the man and woman who were leaving latched the door at once behind them, and only the wheeze of an old melodeon could be heard following them down the rocky overgrown road.

"We left before the fun really started," the wife protested. "You've no idea how good it gets later. Peadar hadn't even warmed up for his step dance and Paid Eoin was only on his second pint. He never begins yarning until he's well into his third one."

"Then we did leave at the right time,' the man grinned. "You know I can't stand those whiskery ancients with their Old Moore's wisdom. You can have them all to yourself tomorrow night," he finished on a coaxing note, and then he realised he'd said more than he had intended at this juncture.

"You mean you won't come out tomorrow night?"

"I mean I won't be here tomorrow night," he said gently, an arm about her waist as he steered her down the hill to the crossroads. "I only came up to say, so to speak, that I couldn't come. I only knew I couldn't yesterday, and you were all expecting me and I thought it was better – "

"Why?"

"O'Kelly isn't satisfied with the price. I must be in town before eleven on Monday morning to see if I can push the deal through. It's possible that it may take several days. I must set off from here after lunch tomorrow."

"I mean why did you come just to say you weren't coming? That was stupid. All those preparations the O'Friels were making – "

"Stuff the O'Friels. I came to see you. Two hundred miles up here and the same back tomorrow, just to see you. I didn't like to write or telegraph."

"It would have been better."

"Look, you're not crying, are you?"

"I'm not crying. But you can tell Mrs O'Friel yourself – I'm not going to. I know you mentioned about this O'Kelly thing in the last letter, but I didn't think it was so important. Is it a woman?"

"Sheila, you're crazy. What the hell would I want with a woman? I've got one."

"If it is a woman, you can take her to beautiful Greece with you, for all I care. No, let me go. I'm going back to the pub, and I'll walk back later with Wee Tommy as I do every other night. Grass widowhood's nothing new to me, remember."

"Wee Tommy will be as drunk as a lord and will probably get sick all over your shoes."

"I'll risk that."

"*I'm sorry*. Won't you believe that I'm sorry."

"I believe you. Think of me on Monday night in town and I'll do you the same favour here. Goodnight. You'll be asleep by the time I get back." Her tone made it clear that this was as she wanted it to be.

Then, more quickly than he had anticipated, she twisted away from him and ran back towards the pub. He followed her slowly for a few steps, and then stopped when the blast of light and sound came again as she lifted the latch. The door closed at once, and he stood for several minutes in the darkness on the stony path, staring at the place where the light had been, listening to the wheeze of the old melodeon. Then he walked back in the direction of the crossroads, cursing softly in the silence that was only broken occasionally by the unseen incoming tide.

You Must Be Joking

Morgan Judge, who had progressed from art to commerce and from wealth to blissful idleness, surveyed his early-morning kitchen with satisfaction. His cat lifted a blue and flattering eye from the warm depths of her basket, the sun seeped gently through yellow curtains, and as yet the tea cosy had not been lifted from the telephone. Even if the instrument did ring it would be with a gentle faraway plea which could easily be disregarded if that moment's precise mood did not warrant lifting first the tea cosy and then the receiver. Normally, of course, you marked the beginning of each day by unveiling the telephone. That was merely custom and not essential: this morning he might not unveil it at all.

Humming a strong passage from one of the Brandenburg Concertos, he flipped back the curtains and surveyed the world. Spring. The unholy clamour of birds, the straight tinted spears of tulips just about to burst into flower, the green lawn moist and beautiful after its first mowing of the year.

Still humming, Morgan filled a miniature silver teapot with water and put it to boil on an electric ring. Kettles he despised. While it boiled, he looked at the multitude of postcards and scribbled reminders which Mona had pinned to the wall behind the telephone.

"Thursday, 6 o'c. Hibernian," he read aloud. "Ask laundry about yellow pillow case, curse them." And then, "8 o'c. Ross, Wed." Yes. That was last night. How are you this morning, Ross Amory? And how, Morgan wondered, is my wife? They didn't share the same bed any more now, and recently they had fixed up separate rooms, but this was merely a civilised arrangement best suited to their circumstances. There were certainly times when Mona irritated him, but on the whole she was the person whose company he found least demanding and most flattering in the world – he had known a little of the world in his time, as he liked to remind people.

When the water boiled he made weak China tea in the miniature teapot and then toasted two slices of rye bread. While it was still warm he spread on the crisp surface about a spoonful of olive oil – not the promiscuous variety, but pure virgin olive oil from a large can, replaced twice a year by a most superior grocer. Each can cost £8, and it was cheap at the price.

As he nibbled, occasionally gyrating oddly to avoid getting a drip of oil on his crimson silk dressing-gown (which had a matching scarf) the Siamese rubbed herself affectionately against his legs as an indication that she would like her morning trip out of doors. He opened the window and decanted her through it, then washed his hands carefully, and was returning with pleasure to his oily toast when the phone bubbled gently beneath the tea cosy. It was more a vibration than an actual noise, and more a memory of one than an actual vibration happening at that moment. On a generous impulse – for this was normally Mona's job – he tossed aside the cosy and picked up the receiver. It was, after all, a rather special day.

"Hello."

"Hello, sir. Patrick Nelson Armstrong here."

"Who?"

"Armstrong of *The Clarion*, sir. Wondering if on this propitious day I might speak to Mona Ambrose. About the plans for her next book perhaps."

"She is asleep," Morgan said severely, "celebrating the publication of her present book. I can't possibly waken her up at ten o'clock in the morning."

"Of course not,' the wretched voice agreed, "but I wonder if she – that is, I wonder if both of you could come along to my hotel – it's the Shelbourne, actually – and have dinner with me this evening? And later perhaps do me the honour of coming along to Tony Tully's new play? It so happens I have been promised three tickets."

"Three tickets," said Morgan, impressed despite himself. The revered president of this island republic could hardly hope to be given more than three tickets for this starry first night. It was even rumoured that the production might go on tour to Cork.

"You see, Tony knows I know something to his credit," the confident voice explained, "and if I let it out his reputation as a bastard would be ruined."

"Tell you what," Morgan offered, "come to the publisher's reception at 6 o'clock in the Hibernian this evening and we'll see. You may even meet my wife there."

"Wonderful. My predecessor told me how charming she is. Perhaps you would be kind enough to look out for a lanky fellow wearing a yellow waistcoat, whom the doorman will probably be in the process of evicting?"

"No need," Morgan said handsomely, "I'll have an invitation sent around to your hotel. Goodbye."

"Thank you so much, sir."

The voice vanished and Morgan returned to his toast and soggy oil. He generously added another slice of rye toast – anointed rather less liberally with pure virgin olive oil – to his wife's repast, and carried up the tray. He did not knock at her bedroom door but, tray carefully balanced, elbowed his way in, and as soon as his hands were free, drew back the curtains vigorously before looking towards the bed.

Mona heaved herself and her yellow duvet in one movement away from the bright sunlight and replaced her face under the warmth. Only her short cropped hair showed, and it reminded him of the knitted dolls one sees sometimes in babies' prams. Once it had been silkily brown and beautiful, but a series of expensive hairdressers had turned it first platinum blond, then red, then a sort of smoky grey, then black, and now brown again. At times indeed, only for the extraordinary fairish streaks (each quite distinct and not intended to blend with the rest, it seemed, but put in at the staggering cost of 75p per streak) she reminded him of the old Mona who used to write bad poetry, and who shattered him on their wedding day by appearing with a cropped boy's head, her romantic long hair having been left at the feet of her first hairdresser the evening before.

He waited for Mona's first wakening groan, and sat down on her dressing stool which was covered in yellow

76

velvet. A big print of Botticelli's "Venus and Mars" shone in the spill of light above the mantelpiece and, as always, he pitied that poor bastard who had laboured and spent himself without taking so much as a feather out of the pert girl sitting up there in bed and shaking out her snake-curled hair. Distracted, he became aware of his annoyance that Mona was staring and half-smiling at him before he had noticed she was awake, and he thumped over with the tray.

"There, madam. Sit and eat."

She was never at her best at such times of the morning. Her night cream had sunk in and so she wasn't greasy, but her brown eyes were so puffy that three hours later nobody would believe what he had seen. She licked her dry lips and smiled at him. From this angle it was obvious that she had two chins, both of them quite attractive. But nobody could say she had not successfully cherished her teeth, which were small and white and pretty as a cat's.

"Did I waken you?" she asked sweetly, reaching up to kiss him. It was a time-honoured opening gambit, at once a reminder of where she had been the previous evening and an expression of meaningless apology. As usual, he didn't answer.

"Happy publication day," he said.

"Oh God!" She crumpled her shoulders and closed her eyes. "I shall never get used to it. I know nothing will happen – nothing ever does. But I always feel the same way. That the publisher will realise his mistake and send over Alan to take all that lovely money away. That I shall be banned by my own countrymen on this very day – but they never ban you any more now, do they? So why do I go on feeling – undefended, at somebody's mercy, abandoned, every single publication day?"

"Because you enjoy the contrast between that and the real thing," Morgan said unfeelingly. "You will be in the hands of your hairdresser in forty-five minutes. You and I and Signor Cicisbeo d'Amato will then have a champagne luncheon, at my expense, in your favourite dive overlooking the river – though indeed I can think of better places."

"How can you call beautiful Ross such a beastly name?" she murmured. "And when may I have just plain butter on my toast?"

"After that," Morgan went on, ignoring her, "we shall go on our customary tour of the bookshops to see which has the smartest display before we take you to Switzers to sign autographs for all those depraved stockbrokers and libidinous elderly civil servants. Then I shall take you home to your waiting bath, while Signor Cicisbeo departs for his, and then you will spend two hours preparing for the reception at which you will arrive (as usual) forty-five minutes late. Today, however, you'd better be a little sharper. Armstrong of *The Clarion* is over to see you, and he'll be there."

"You're such a lamb chop," she said affectionately. "What would I do without you? Any telegrams?"

"I left them as usual – in the hall to encourage you to come down. One from your publishers – with love, no doubt. One from Signor Cicisbeo d'Amato – ditto, no doubt. And one from the milkman, like last time."

"Ordinary people are so sweet to me," Mona sighed emotionally, drinking the last of the tea and struggling to finish up one slice of the oiled toast. She did not quite succeed, and handed up the tray apologetically, her lips greasy. Morgan took it away downstairs to give to his cat.

The reception, for which two enormous ground-level rooms had been booked, was much the same as last year's and all the years before. There were cascades of Spring flowers on the buffet table (all twenty-five of Mona's books had been launched in Spring) and champagne which the waiters had been instructed not to allow flow too freely, and cheese dip and smoked salmon and a boar's head which was probably made of plaster. Certainly it looked plaster, Morgan decided, no more real than most of the guests.

There was a huddle of poets, over beside the Bushmills – two of them happy homosexuals, one still-hopeful womaniser, and three irrefutably married, with large families. One of these was given to ceaseless debunking of Yeats in the hope of tidying him finally out of the way to make room for himself. The three wives stood together, two of them very pretty and very pregnant; the other extremely large by nature. She was an authority on Charlotte Brooke, although few in the room could precisely recall who Charlotte Brooke had been.

There were novelists, rather more gregarious than the poets, all over the place. Some were dressed in open tartan shirts because this was traditionally a very dressy affair and it was a symbol of independence, universally respected, to wear no tie. Many of the tieless ones were better novelists whose own works quietly appeared in the bookshops without the aid of any rituals like this, but some were television people who had come straight from the overheated studios. Above one of the Adam fireplaces was a large blown-up print of Mona prising open a crocus with two fingers, her tongue held between her teeth.

Underneath stood Ross Amory, heavy dark head thrown back in a manner that recalled a film star of the 'thirties. His spade-shaped black beard was very contemporary, however, and recalled that of Shakespeare. The most remarkable thing about it was that it was composed of a number of small tight curls, rather like Persian lamb. His finely preserved large white teeth flashed amiably around, while his dark and splendid eyes skimmed the entrances where Mona might at any moment appear. Once, as a student, Morgan remembered, Ross had published a tiny gilt-edged volume of translations from Ovid, at the expense of his mother, who had never actually read them but who still kept house for him and was willing to pay for the publication of anything further he might add to his output. But these days he preferred to concentrate on his widely successful one-man show assembled from Yeats.

As Morgan went off to fetch a drink for a large lady journalist who was well known for her hatred of Mona Ambrose, a tall blond young man in the tightest trousers he had ever seen went up to Ross. "May I introduce myself, sir? Armstrong of *The Clarion*. I spoke to you on the telephone this morning, if you remember?"

"You spoke to me on the telephone this morning – I remember quite distinctly," Morgan cut in. "How do you do. Let me get you a drink."

"How do you do, sir? I do beg your pardon. A tincture of Irish whiskey would be very pleasant if it's available." He was bowing in apology to Ross when Morgan introduced them.

'This is the poet Ross Amory, a friend of ours."

"How do you do, sir."

Ross merely vouchsafed a flash of his beautiful teeth before turning away to speak to the lady journalist. His very deep honeyed voice kept her happy until Morgan returned with the drinks, by which time the *Clarion* man had vanished. Annoyed, they glanced around for him until Ross (who could see around comers when he chose) picked him out at the far end of the room, in the process of kissing Mona's hand.

There was a sudden drift of people towards that end of the room, but Morgan banged the young man's glass down on the mantelpiece and decided to stay put. The disapproval on Ross Amory's face amused him. "Very pleasant young fella, don't you think," Morgan said wickedly, and affected surprise at Ross's reaction.

"I think he suffers from one of the worst defects of his class, ignorance of its own insignificance," Ross murmured, and stared across the sea of heads to the tall blond one bent over Mona's. The fellow was even taller than he was, and Ross was accustomed to looking down on most people in Dublin. He somehow contrived to look down at Patrick Nelson Armstrong when Mona brought him over, by directing his gaze down along the patrician length of his nose and examining only the newsman's top waistcoat button. The waistcoat itself, he noted, was of canary handwoven tweed and indescribably vulgar.

"Would you believe it, darling, both sets of Patrick's grandparents were Irish!" prattled Mona happily, squeezing an elbow of Ross and Morgan at the same time. "He says he felt at home here right from the beginning. Did you know his children are called Devorgilla, Conall and Caitriona – isn't that sweet?"

"Charming," Ross agreed, without lifting an eyebrow, and smiling benignly at Mona.

"Something in me snaps back into place when I come over here," Patrick offered eagerly. "I feel as if they misplaced a vital component when I was assembled over there, and it's only when I touch down on Irish soil that suddenly – whatever it is, rights itself."

"Whereabouts on your person do you feel this error of assembly when you are over there?" Ross enquired softly, lifting his eyes in apparent candour to the younger man's face. But Mona was not deceived.

"Stop it at once, Ross," she said.

"Where is your wife?" Morgan cut in peaceably. "Forgive my enquiry, but nobody mentioned her."

"Virginia isn't up to travel just at present," Patrick said modestly.

"Poor thing," Mona smiled, "What will you call this one?"

"Stella if it's a girl – because of Swift, you know. I thought of Diarmuid if it's a boy."

"Doesn't your wife have any say in the choice of names?" Ross asked insolently.

"Her father was Irish," Patrick smiled. His good humour seemed unbreakable. "The only people who object to the children's names are the teachers of the elder two, Devorgilla and Conall. The poor teachers can't pronounce them."

"Nor can you, as a matter of fact." Ross's coup de

grace was delivered effectively just before he sauntered across the room to talk to a fellow-poet.

Mona cleared her throat nervously. "Ross isn't feeling himself today – you must excuse him, Patrick. He's overtired."

"Of course. Poets are moody chaps."

"Let me get you some more Irish," Morgan said suddenly as though in amends. "Bushmills?"

"Oh, if you please."

"You, Mona?"

"Bushmills for me too, please."

When Morgan returned, Mona thanked him so profusely that he looked closely at her.

"Something awfully unfortunate has happened, darling," she said, giving him her most dependent smile. "Patrick was absolutely promised three seats for Tony's play tonight, and just after lunch they rang his hotel and said he could only have two. So you must go, darling."

"Don't be silly." Morgan knew her so well that this speech seemed to him not only charming but touchingly funny. "You know perfectly well that you wouldn't miss this for any money, and you know equally well that if I did decide to go, Patrick might find that he had, after all, only been allowed one ticket."

"I assure you, sir, upon my honour – "

"I'm joking, of course," Morgan said kindly. "Naturally Mona will go."

"You're sure you don't mind?" Mona insisted.

"Not a bit. You've saved me yet another version of Tony's unappetising childhood and early seduction by his elderly father."

"Then thank you, Patrick, I'll give my publisher the slip and I'll come."

"The honour is entirely mine," Patrick was solemnly assuring her as Morgan left them.

He was gathering up two forgotten signed volumes of *Games My Mother* Taught Me after most of the guests had gone, when Ross appeared with his dark face thunderstruck.

"Where has Mona gone?"

"To Tony Tully's first night with Fleet Street's crack Arts man."

"Gone alone? You mean unaccompanied? You actually mean to say you let her – "

"She's gone to the theatre accompanied by that nice young fellow Irishman to whom you were exceedingly rude."

"You can't mean it. You must be joking."

"Of course I'm not joking. Didn't you hear he's safely married with children who have names of impeccable respectability? Don't you know the full-page coverage he will give to Mona in the Arts section of next Sunday's Clarion? Have you any remotest idea of what that coverage will mean to Mona in terms of copies sold?"

"I think you're simply disgusting," Ross burst out, 'thinking in terms of sordid royalties when the honour of your wife is at stake. I know his kind. He has the ferret's eyes of a rapist and he comes from the most depraved city in the world. How could you expose her to positive moral danger?"

As he raged, and Morgan, with the skill of long practice, patiently tried to soothe him down, Mona was settling contentedly into the dress circle with Patrick.

"You must call me Lisa," she smiled.

"That's what I love about Irish people. You're so natural and unaffected," said Patrick Nelson Armstrong.

Lord of the Back Seat

A love affair with a married woman seemed, by its very nature, to promise a certain stability. It was very different from office involvements which perished quickly in the boredom of the day's comings and goings. This affair was more protected and romantic, the stuff of the very best French fiction. I had, after all, fallen in love with poor doomed Emma Bovary long before I left the small town where I grew up. Emma had simply been unfortunate in the bad egg she had chosen to love. I would never take advantage of a vulnerable woman like that. Aileen, in any case, had never even pretended to be a vulnerable woman.

She was very unlike any of the girls I knew at home or at the bank, the crudity of whose advances could never be mistaken. She wasn't, of course, a girl. She might have been thirty-six or seven when I was twenty, although I was never quite sure. One day she had been sent to me with a cheque for five hundred Deutschmarks and she wanted to know what to do with it. Could she lodge it to her account here or did she have to go to College Green and get it changed there? I told her I could change it for her, that I was in fact the Foreign Exchange Department of this small branch office. She smiled and said I didn't look like a department of any kind. When I asked her what she thought a department should look like she smiled fractionally and said "Older."

Her name was Aileen O'Malley and whether she had foreign exchange problems or not she always came to me after that. I began actually to look forward to her visits. One day, a few seconds before closing time, she rushed in with rain flowing in rivulets down a white raincoat. After I'd cashed a cheque for her she offered me a lift home with quite casual kindness. I explained that a banker has two hours work ahead of him after the public has been disposed of and she smiled regretfully. "Poor you."

It was still pouring rain at five o'clock when I stood on the top step fastening up my anorak and looking down at a scene of greater traffic confusion than usual. I became aware of a klaxon blasting away in the middle of the bottleneck and there she was smiling through the open door of her car, beckoning me. I made a dash for it, through furiously hooting motorists and I brought rivers of rain into the car with me but she didn't seem to mind. "So happens I'm on my way back from delivering someone at his music lesson," she smiled. "Fortunate accident that I saw you." That was the beginning.

After she had left me a little over a year later I had grown to know her and her family so well that knowing she was gone was like losing a book you have more than half-read, whose ending you have been saving up and now will never know. It wasn't that I ever knew them individually very well, though I went to a few parties at the house, and two or three cheerful family suppers. It was that in the course of talking with her several evenings a week for long hours at a stretch, their problems had become partly mine, as I believed mine had become wholly hers. I knew which of the five children had a stammer and which used to sleepwalk to the terror of everybody whenever he was worried about school. I knew the name of each succeeding boyfriend of the charming fifteen-year-old Fiona, and I knew that the twin girls must never be separated because each complemented the other and so was miserable in her absence. Best of all, I knew Stephen, their father – his habit of shattering things by an incautious movement, his nervous cough which so irritated Aileen, his patience with the children, his occasional bouts of drunkenness. She was not, I think, a particularly good talker, yet she somehow described him so well that when I finally met him it was as though I had known him long ago except for one thing. He was much younger than I'd imagined – her own age in fact. His brown and shaggy hair gave him the look of a good-natured dog. His eyes were like that too, and I felt slightly ashamed of knowing more than I ought about him. "We lie together like two Crusaders on a tomb", she told me when I'd only known her three days. Yet five children? The youngest however was seven – the sleepwalker.

She surprised me sometimes with phrases like that. Two Crusaders on a tomb. She was not allusive as a rule and she had read no more than you would expect a girl to have read who married at twenty after a brief and I must say undistinguished career on the stage. Her largest part had been lady-in-waiting to Gertrude the Queen (no lines) but her roles became more important when she broke at last into advertising. She was, she told me, the woman whose children brought seventeen friends home to lunch because she had a habit of serving a certain brand of instant dessert on Tuesdays. She was also the girl whose change of deodorant saved her marriage. Her sense of humour, to my great joy, began to improve under my tutelage. When I first knew her she would give these facts straight, with some pride. She was particularly pleased, for instance, about that first time she wore a shawl and petticoats and was the sort of friendly Irish girl who would welcome you a hundred thousand times to a genuine Irish thatched cottage at a reasonable rent per week to include central heating. The advertisement had been shown to a club of wealthy businessmen in Dusseldorf and twice in Amsterdam. Several of our embassies had copies of it.

I can't quite remember the point at which she ceased to be a marvellous joke, not quite credible, a whim of the gods. I can remember the stage when I never did believe she would turn up next time, but that quickly passed. She rapidly became, or so I believed, essential – her too-loud laugh, her crazy optimism, the way she would fill the dingy room by the canal bridge with apples from her garden and news of her children. She would listen with absolute attention to my own bank politics, my prospects of promotion, my swollen dreams of becoming known as a poet. Best of all, she would listen when I read to her, and now and again, apart from saying, "It's lovely – I love it," she would say what was better, "I don't like the third line – it sticks out like a sore thumb, like ..." She would then dissolve in laughter, but she would be right. I never did understand where the embryonic critical faculty came from, but it was there. It was there when she bothered to use it. It was precious because I knew nobody else to whom I could profitably read anything.

There was something else I didn't understand either and that was physical. The very first afternoon, with the rain lashing away outside and the gas fire bubbling and spluttering in my room, there was a moment of silence as she bent to take off a soaked sandal when I didn't like the freckly dimpled forearm with its golden hairs or the slightly thickened wrists. Without speaking I said No, but that became nonsense a few moments later, and remained nonsense for more than a year. Sexually she was exuberant and inventive, a little overpowering. So restless with life herself, she had lain, perhaps, too long beside her dead Crusader on his tomb, although the tomb itself was extremely comfortable. So she said. She would like to share it some time with me, she said, instead of using my two-foot-six divan with the broken spring. I assumed her to be joking.

Rainy September became a golden warm October and I wrote something which pleased me. The night I had hoped to read it to her she didn't turn up, but she rang me on a faint crackling line at ten o'clock. The weather was so lovely they had all gone down for the weekend to the cottage. This was the first I had heard of a cottage. She wanted me to take the first train down in the morning if I didn't mind using a sleeping bag and dossing down on a bunk in the boys' room.

"Even if I had thought of it in time you wouldn't have fitted in the car with seven of us," she laughed, and I felt this was going too far. I refused the invitation and pointed out that I would have been quite satisfied if she had just remembered to phone me to say she couldn't come that evening. There was a long surprised pause and then a gentle good-night.

I had often wondered about the type of woman who calmly incorporates a lover into the family circle (Bernard Shaw's mother was one of them) but when I met one, at last, she fitted into no category. She was certainly managing, yet resigned when firmly opposed. She was neither cold-blooded nor merely in search of convenient comfort. She seemed devoted to her family and me in apparently sensible proportions. If her husband (of whom she seemed to be quite fond) had been sexually ardent it is possible that she would never have offered me that lift home, but having done so she faced the realities of the situation in a way that was not very easy for me.

Next weekend, for instance, there was a change forecast in the weather, so she informed her husband that she would drive down alone to clean up after the summer and do some essential minor maintenance before forgetting about the cottage until next year. I accompanied her with the greatest misgivings, which proved well-founded.

The place was about seventy miles out of town, a pleasant long bungalow made of brick and cedar wood and designed, she told me, by her husband. It and an immensely ugly office block in town were the only examples of his work I ever saw; there could hardly have been less resemblance between the two. Approached by a sandy track off the road from the nearest village, the bungalow nestled without any disturbance among its sandhills. Angles of roof or gable followed the lines of the sandhills themselves, and facing it was a golden beach empty except for a few cows. They drank from a small freshwater stream which came down from the hills to end its course in the salty ocean. It was six o'clock on a Friday evening, I remember, and full tide. The water stretched calm and glittering and dark blue as far as Rosslare. The weather forecasters had evidently been mistaken. A swim seemed the most desirable thing in the world though most of the beach was in shadow.

"The water won't be cold," she promised me. "It will have soaked up all the heat of the last few weeks. You'll see."

I didn't see, but by that time it hardly mattered. I noticed that inside the house she had fingered with some surprise a bulky leather camera-case lying beside a small piece of female luggage on the kitchen table, though she made no comment when the back door leading to the beach proved to be open. I knew in my bones what we would find, and so we did. A man and a girl, both heavily tanned, lay in one another's arms against the sand dunes, in the last pool of sunshine.

Aileen at once ran shouting towards them, calling impatiently to me when I held back. They were not in the least put out by the interruption – as pleased as she was, it seemed, to discover one another. She introduced them as Harry Lane and Sheila Meehan and me also, simply by name, without explanation. He was heavily middle-aged and swarthy, with a throaty laugh and friendly dark eyes. She seemed a mere schoolgirl, leggy and blonde and inclined to giggle.

"We had absolutely no idea we'd find any of you here," the girl said. "Is everybody down?"

"Only ourselves," Aileen assured them, and I intensely disliked the inclusive phrasing. It seemed that friends often used the cottage at odd times by open invitation. A second key could always be picked up from the cleaning-woman in the village. None of this I had known before, and now quite suddenly I wanted to get away.

"Excuse me, I'd like a swim before it's too cold," I said, and the girl Sheila, goose-pimply by now, snuggled up to the man and shuddered. The last medallion of sun had narrowed around them.

It was quite a few minutes later when Aileen joined me in the icy water. I was swimming by this time, not so paralysed by cold as when I had hovered for a while before plunging. Aileen waded straight out and then dived in head first as soon as she got sufficient depth. She came up beside me spluttering and breathless.

"You'll like them," she gasped. "Harry's a very clever cameraman – going to do a small job tomorrow as a matter of fact when his assistant Michael comes down with the rest of the gear."

"You knew this?" I asked incredulously.

"Not at all. But since I'm here and he could do with another female he's offered me a job. Said he'd be glad if you'd stand in too – already working on another composition. Will you? It can be amusing – very."

"Prostitute my person, such as it is, for a television ad? You must be crazy, Aileen."

"Don't be so stuffy." I suddenly felt years older than she was as she laughed at me before swimming powerfully away. I was happy to dog-paddle in the opposite direction. It was very cold.

It remained chilly for the evening in fact. I had expected to find the touches of domesticity painful – forgotten toys, perhaps, colouring books half-finished after some rainy day, a tweed jacket belonging to Stephen hanging up as a symbol of moral right. But it wasn't like that at all. There was hilarious joint cooking of a substantial meal, stories and jokes about people I'd never heard of, a long anecdote about the hitch they'd got to the village because Harry's car had suffered a relapse of recent engine trouble, and then a mass bundling into Aileen's station wagon for a few drinks at somebody's favourite pub. It was called The Harvester and it had a thatched roof and cartwheels outside, but inside were a ballad group from Wexford whose amplification would have been sufficient to fill the National Stadium. We went from The Harvester to a few other places similarly equipped, which left me with a screaming headache by the time we got back. Nobody had any aspirins – there was, however, an old bottle of Junior Aspirin on the bathroom shelf with one abandoned pink pill in it.

I had wondered vaguely about the mechanics of going to bed, but they proved simplicity itself. Whatever inhibitions there might have been had drowned quietly a few hours previously in the alcohol. Except mine. I was reminded of the occasions before I left home when a friend could manage to borrow his father's car and we would take out two girls to a dance twenty miles away. There was a boreen close to our town where Maurice would pull in the car on the way home. Although he would have been at a physical disadvantage in the front, it was from there the contented sounds of complete isolation always came. Lord of the back seat, I would be immobilised by embarrassment, to the amazement and sometimes annoyance of the girl.

Now in the comfortable main bedroom of the cottage it was the same. Sounds of laughter came from the other room, the scraping of something along the floor. "In there," Aileen giggled, "there are two single divans. I think they are about to be made one."

Here again was an example of her occasional felicitous turn of phrase. About to be made one.

"What's the matter, baby?" She was undressed by now, copper brown in the spill of light from the bedside lamp. She appeared to be wearing a minute white two-piece swim suit – the only two pieces of her body normally covered when she lay in the sun. The effect usually amused and touched me. I thought of them as my two pieces, but not tonight.

"I told you I have a headache," I mumbled. "A pretty lousy one, as a matter of fact."

"If only I'd been more provident," she wailed, embracing me. "What other house would you find entirely without aspirins? You must go to sleep my love. I'll probably waken you up in the middle of the night and your headache will be gone by then. Yes?"

"If you can waken me," I said sourly. She put out the light and went to open the curtains. A far brighter light from the harvest moon poured in. Glancing out, my eyes were hurt by the metallic dazzle of the sea.

"If we were swimming now," she said, "every stroke

would send a shower of silver coins shooting out from our fingertips. Have you ever seen it?"

"Never."

"Some time," she smiled, and came to bed.

Scrupulously fair, she kissed me kindly and rolled away to the far edge from which in a matter of ten minutes or so I heard her quiet breathing. There was, as it happened, no moonlight awakening.

In the first daylight – cold-looking and misty now over the swinging full tide – I got up carefully and dressed. I scribbled a note explaining that after all I found I couldn't face the gregarious day. Asking her forgiveness, I signed my initial and crept away. She sighed and stirred when I opened the bedroom door but did not waken. Neither, of course, did anybody else.

It was grey and cool outside with a small breeze coming in from the sea. My headache was gone. The sense of liberation was acutely enjoyable. Somewhere a curlew cried in the distance and he was answered by another and then by a flotilla of seagulls. I turned to look at them bobbing like ducks on the full tide, swaying toy-like to and fro. The cows of yesterday had disappeared. I had a sudden impulse to swim by myself, but that would have been asking for trouble. Instead I set off down the sandy track, stopping only at a pit which had recently been dug to bury dozens of whiskey bottles. They lay like dead fish against the slope of the pit and I wondered if the grave had been left open to bury more or if Stephen had tired of the task.

Brooding about this I turned along the empty road to the village and walked at a fast clip, enjoying the crunch of my own feet in the frequent patches of gravel. When a milk lorry clattered nearby I thumbed a lift into Enniscorthy and thence by bus back to the city, still locked dustily in its Indian summer.

The relationship somehow survived this and many another setback. In the spring I had a poem published on the literary page of a Dublin newspaper and Aileen was immensely proud. Its dedication was "For A", because (and it was probably the reason for its acceptance) she had caused me to rewrite four of the lines. In the late summer I spent three moribund weeks with the maiden aunts who had reared me, and long before I went back to work I regretted refusing her invitation to spend part of the holiday at the cottage.

"How would you explain me to Stephen?" I had asked.

"A friend of mine needs no explanation, " she had smiled patiently, but it hadn't seemed possible. To go swimming with the children, take part in family outings here or there, and sleep (perhaps with her occasionally when Stephen was in town) on the studio couch in a locked living-room – it didn't seem possible. When I said so she smiled impatiently this time and said how stupid of me. If I joined the family it would certainly not be, for the time being, as her lover but as a friend. I would sleep alone on the studio couch, or on a bunk in the boys' room, anywhere – on the beach if I liked. I thought of the cheerful young Fiona and of the possible presence of her newest boyfriend, of the discussions at night whose style would be taken from the school debating hall, the clamouring of the twins for a story, the trustful face of

Ciaran the sleepwalker, and it all seemed in the most appallingly bad taste.

I said so, and that evening she left early, thoughtful. I ran after her and reminded her that it was I who would suffer from her absence and she smiled but said nothing.

Almost exactly a year after the rainy September day when she had first come to the flat, I cleaned and dusted and cooked a beef Stroganoff from the Robert Carrier book I'd recently acquired. She had expressed delight at the prospect of my cooking for her. Certainly, with wine and candles and a gigantic melon marinated in brandy, all looked tempting enough, but eventually I ate alone that evening. Seven-thirty passed and eight and nine and ten, and then I sat down to the table. She had not even phoned.

The explanation when it came seemed almost adequate – an old friend of the family, Bartley, or some such name, had dropped in. He had spent ten years working on the Toronto Globe and Mail and now was home to stay, looking twenty years older and not ten. Fiona remembered him since the time she was a baby. There had been an impromptu celebration when he had just walked in with presents for everybody, and if she had thought I would accept she would certainly have phoned to invite me. This I knew to be true, though I don't understand why she couldn't have phoned anyway.

We somehow survived this too, though nothing was ever quite the same again. Maybe it was my fault. Resentment over the uneaten meal (to which I had never subsequently made the slightest reference) rankled for a long time. So did the fact that she no longer wanted to see me regularly. She would phone unexpectedly and say "I'm coming – OK?" and it was, but one could no longer look forward to the joy of seeing her on any special evening. It shouldn't particularly have mattered since I seldom went out anyhow, except now and again alone to the theatre, but it did.

Early in the new year (for whose commencement I had attended a large and cheerful party at her house) her phone calls became less and less frequent, although when we did meet everything seemed just as good as ever. She was no less ardent or attentive than she had ever been and she was even more interested in what I might have written since last time. When occasionally an evening failed it was always my fault, due to pent-up resentment and the changed pattern of our days. There was another odd thing which worried me. She never came to the bank anymore, and when I questioned her about this she passed it off lightly. It was more convenient to go to our head office since she was often in town to lunch these days. Some time or other however, she'd surprise me by just walking in. That was one promise she certainly did keep.

I think what I eventually felt most that spring, apart from the physical deprivation, was having nobody who would listen with absolute attention to the minor worries of work, the occasional sting of literary ambition, nobody in fact who would listen to anything I wanted to talk about. When I heard a promotion vacancy was about to arise in a provincial branch office I wanted to talk to her about that, but she hadn't phoned for two weeks, and then it had been only for a few minutes – chat of the children, which I was delighted to hear. But the doorbell rang (she said) before I had had a chance to say more than a few words myself, and I had to be content with the promise of an invitation to join them all for a meal soon.

Two more weeks passed. The young civil servant in the flat below asked me in for coffee one evening and in appreciation I took her to the theatre. She was twenty-two, happy, blonde and beautiful. The play was excellent.

I have seldom been so bored in my life. Next evening when Aileen rang, my hand shook as I held the phone but I made myself take the initiative I had seldom taken before. I asked her to come over, mumbled something about my new-found skill in cooking, and listened in agony as the long pause lengthened to the point of incredulity that she could still be at the other end of the line.

She was. She said, "I can't. Believe me it just isn't possible. It's very difficult to explain on the phone but I'm no longer free. Please try and understand!"

"You mean the stone effigy of a Crusader can suddenly sit up and join the human race again?"

"Something like that." She laughed slightly at the fact, I thought then, that I hadn't forgotten her image and then she invited me over for a meal. I said I'd come. She asked me to bring any new poems I'd written. She couldn't wait to read them.

After that happy evening, during which she shone among her own family with a kindlier light than I had ever remembered, especially when Stephen came in with a loaded briefcase and a murmured excuse, I made an appalling blunder. Loneliness, the exhilaration of watching her approve of what I had written and (once again) putting her finger on a weak line that had to go, the imagined relapse of Stephen, a painful reminder of the response of my own body to hers – what was it? What insane error of judgement caused me to write her a passionate letter next day and then post the cursed thing instead of killing it against the bars of my gas fire like all the others?

Two days later I walked home along the muddy canal banks greening already with another spring and I thought, if I stay out long enough before stepping into the dingy hall her letter will be there, crisp and blue among the circulars, the electricity bills, the postcards, the sad flotsam and jetsam of other people's lives in a big house full of small flats. But even though I lingered over a beer in Henry Grattan's pub, even though by the time I got in somebody else had laid out the afternoon's post on the hall table, there was nothing for me. There were the bills and the circulars and an airmail letter for the lovely girl in the downstairs flat and a postcard from Miami and the same crumpled grey envelope marked URGENT for the fellow who had gone away six months previously, but there was nothing for me.

It was worse on the four following days. I would come in and find my name on top of two or three pieces of post. I would carry them upstairs and leave them untouched on the table. If I didn't look before I had finished eating, before washing up, before seven o'clock, it might be there. It was not. There was a bill from the dentist, notices of preservationist activities, a letter from my aunts, a long manila envelope containing four rejected poems with his compliments from the editor of a little magazine (I had sent them to him two years ago).

Then I started wondering if she had received the letter, if I had addressed it properly, if her husband had perhaps opened it. This was the worst time of all. What I simply couldn't face then was the probability that she had received it, read it – and decided to do nothing whatever about it. I could have understood her writing a two-line reply, reproving me or expressing regret or anger or refusal to read any more letters. At this stage I would have been most grateful of all for the sort of insincerities and exaggerations often used on such occasions. I would have submitted with good grace to being told how I could never be forgotten, how nothing could ever break the bond between us. It shows I suppose what a low ebb one can sink to at such times. But I got nothing. Not a line or a phone call or any slightest acknowledgement of my sufferings.

One evening the girl downstairs asked me in to watch a play on her hired television set, and the first face I saw when I stepped into the room was Aileen's. The shock was considerable. There she was doing a young mother and daughter act with the leggy blonde girl of that horrible weekend. There was the same beach, her own bungalow in the background, a few athletic men (of whom I supposed I might have been one), an explosion of foam close to the cameras. What were they selling? The swim suits, the beach, the oil responsible for their tanned bodies, the frozen food they would make a tasty meal out of in five minutes back at the bungalow? My cultured hostess had naturally turned down the sound and so I never learned. I closed my eyes on their fade-out smiles and didn't open them again until a mug of coffee was gently placed in my frozen hands.

It was soon after this, towards the end of March, that I phoned her one evening. Maybe blaming her had become so unbearable that I began for a change to blame myself. She had made her decision, told me frankly why she couldn't see me any more (what action could be more honourable than that?) and what had I done? After that letter, for God's sake, what else could she do but ignore it? There were only two replies you could make to a letter like that. She had made the tough one, as she had a perfect right to do, having decided already that the affair must end. So what? So I had to do the civilised thing and phone to apologise however difficult it might be.

It wasn't even difficult in the end. I stood uncomfortably in the draughty hall, hoping that nobody would pass in or out while I was speaking to her, and nobody did. Her voice was kind and understanding. She asked me to hold on while she carried the phone to a quieter place. Then she said she hadn't replied because she thought such insensitivity on her part would be better for me in the end. It might make me resent or hate her and hasten my recovery. She said I was twenty-two (didn't I know?) and it was such a good age. I would find somebody more worthy and also free and I would be happy. We would, she said, always be friends, always be on a special wavelength for all the rest of our lives.

After that she rang often, and chatted freely about anything and everything, especially about her family. I found myself speaking to her (often to the fury of the other residents) for as long as an hour at a time, sometimes even reading poems to her and profiting from her comments. She said she had better not ask me to the house for the moment – it would be better for me. Sometime we would meet, perhaps when I had a girl to bring with me. When

I questioned her about Stephen I fancied I could see her smiling. The transformation was complete – they were very happy. He no longer brought home work and shut himself up with it late into the small hours, she said. His drinking bouts were a thing of the past, she said.

She came striding into the bank one blazing June day in a white dress which accentuated the remembered tan of last year. With her was a man of rather impressive appearance, tall, brown-skinned and silver-haired, a young-looking fifty perhaps. Together they reminded me of jet-set people in a T. V. commercial. She was cheerful and friendly as she introduced him to me, at the same time as she reached into his breast pocket for a better pen than the bank provided. He was Kevin Bartley, she said, a very old friend of the family – perhaps she had mentioned him before?

He was now home for good from Canada to settle down. He had interesting plans for his retirement, she said, including the launching of a literary magazine. At this she actually winked at me unnoticed and then smiled, as though she had just given me a secret present. Scribbling busily, she said we would all meet again soon before the summer was too advanced – as soon as she got back from Greece. Was Stephen going too? She glanced up quickly and said he unfortunately couldn't get away – much too busy at the office. I glanced routinely at her passport, slid her travellers' cheques across the counter to her and wished her a good holiday. With difficulty I suppressed an impulse to wish them both a good holiday.

When they had gone I went to the coffee room but couldn't hold the cup for the shaking of my hands. I

104

remembered now when I had first heard about this Kevin Bartley, the night I'd cooked the meal and she hadn't come because some old friend had just walked in out of the blue-wasn't that it? Quite soon afterwards the dead Crusader had sat up suddenly in his tomb. Why hadn't I realised that the dead don't rise again, not in this life?

It was high summer when I left Dublin. The provincial town of my promotion was almost identical with the one of my birth – a tree-lined mall, seventeen pubs, an air of kindly and resigned stagnation. I welcomed it as eagerly as five years previously I had welcomed escape from all this to the capital. I had said in that unforgotten letter (fully believing it to be true), "I carry you hidden in my bloodstream like some virus awaiting its time and you will never go away," but it wasn't quite true. Physically she did go away so positively that at times I had to remind myself why there was nothing I now wanted to do, nobody I wanted to see. The people who did not go away (and who are with me still) are her children whom I hardly knew at all and her husband whom I feel at last I know only too well.

The Open House

Once again the bell went jangling unanswered through the house. Once again Teresa wandered down the steps, and looked through into the book-walled room. This time, glasses stood about here and there, there were books on the floor, and several large bright pottery ashtrays, loaded with cigarette ends. It was a long room, and Teresa pushed her face against the glass to see through the back window and out into the garden. All she could see were the long waxen buds of a magnolia tree and a stretch of lawn and beyond that a greenhouse with (she was almost certain) a figure bent down inside it.

She ran around to the other side of the steps, past another bay window with drawn curtains, and on to a small yellow door which might lead through to the back garden. Half fearfully, she pushed it open, amazed that it was not locked. She followed a little stony path through the massed crocus beds and tiny dwarf fir trees to the greenhouse. A dumpy elderly woman straightened up angrily and came out with her arms full of forced pink sticks of rhubarb.

"Well?" she said to Teresa, small eyes unfriendly in a pudgy pale face.

"Well, I couldn't get an answer, you see, and I came about the house."

"You can't see anybody about the house now – such a time to knock people up." Her small inquisitive eyes passed over the thin pink tweed coat and down to the white stockings which Teresa suddenly felt must be laddered, "and what would you be wanting to know about the house?"

Teresa lost her temper. "It is advertised for sale, you know. The address is given. And I came here yesterday afternoon and there was nobody in then either."

"So it was you yesterday, too?" the old face giggled. "Knocking fit to raise the dead." Teresa remembered the glasses in the convivial front room and felt very certain that this was a servant, not the owner, despite her air of assurance.

"Can you tell me when I could find the owner at home?"

"There's at home and at home in it," mumbled the old woman. "Ask me, and I'll tell you they're mad sorry already they put the place up for sale at all. All this will blow over, if you ask me."

"I can see it's no use asking you anything," said Teresa, and marched off in good order with her head high.

That evening after supper she persuaded Tom out with her. His interest in acquiring a house and crippling overheads was minimal, and he felt in fact quite satisfied with the cosy poky flat they rented for forty pounds a week. But Teresa's four sisters each had a bright box in the suburbs of Dublin and she dreamed of dazzling them with something different. To Tom she kept making references to the future family and the necessity of providing a room for every boy and girl. When he looked at her satirically over well-polished glasses, as he did now, she frequently burst into tears; but he never paid any attention so it never lasted long.

That evening, eventually, they gained entry. The door was opened by a tall abstracted-looking man in a knitted cardigan, who escorted them from room to room as though he were standing in for somebody else.

"Nice little box, this," he said, indicating what was clearly a maid's room at ground level. "Guaranteed to keep the working classes where they belonged – far away from the family. A girl could easily freeze to death down here with the minimum of inconvenience to everybody else. No fireplace, you see. No room for a wardrobe – she wouldn't have owned much apart from aprons anyway. They went in here."

He pulled open a small wall cupboard, and pointed to the suitcases lying about. "Matter of fact, we've used it as a box room since the last girl went. That was about thirty years ago; in my father's day. Our present housekeeper, who dates from just after the girl's time, has occupied for years the best bedroom in the house."

He had a high pedantic voice and warm friendly blue eyes. His forehead was high and his head pear-shaped, dotted here and there with fuzz like that on an Easter chicken. He led them, vaguely making sounds of approval, from this to the breakfast room which had another queer oil painting above the fireplace, and on to the kitchen, so dazzling, so modern, so warm (despite the unfriendly presence of the greenhouse woman) that

Teresa was rendered speechless by her desire to own it.

Tom had closed up completely and allowed himself to be steered along slightly worn but magnificent carpets up the curved staircase to the drawing-room. Teresa plucked him to notice the Waterford chandeliers, the velvet curtains, the auctioneers' showpieces on all sides. He grunted. He grunted again over the sunken pink bath and the black tiles, over the Georgian cheval glass in the second largest bedroom, and the nudes in heavy gilt frames.

"Don't fancy the Rubens type myself," their guide was saying. "All breasts and buttocks. Now look at this Manet. Different kettle of fish entirely, don't you see. Voluptuous but bony. By which I mean one is aware of the bones."

Tom examined the young girl in the painting and thought she looked no better than she should but (as the man said) considerably better than the buxom bathing beauties. He didn't know what to make of the black cat at her bare heels, so he laughed, the first sign of life from him since they entered the house.

Coming out of the room he hissed to Teresa, "Put this house out your mind, my lady. You'd buy the Mansion House for less."

Downstairs, in the book-walled room that had first attracted Teresa, they were surprised to find a crowd. There had been no sounds of a party in progress, and it was clear why. If this was a party it was the oddest one she had ever seen.

Young men lay about on the carpet, now and again lifting a book off the shelves and holding a consultation about it. A girl in jeans was clipping her toenails in front of the log fire, and a husband and wife (of course?) conducted a fierce though largely silent battle over near the stacked paintings.

All had drinks in various stages of consumption and all looked as comfortably unconcerned as though they lived here.

"Let me introduce you to Colin Healy," said their guide carelessly, and afterwards went to fetch them a drink. Teresa controlled herself with some difficulty and poked Tom surreptitiously.

"Hello," said Colin Healy, getting up politely off the carpet and bowing to Teresa. To her disappointment, he excused himself almost immediately and disappeared through the door. Teresa poked Tom again.

"Did you hear who he is?" she whispered. "I know it's the same because I've seen his pictures heaps of times."

"What about it?" Tom muttered. "Let's get out of here now."

"We have to wait for the drinks. He's gone to get them."

Tom shrugged and sat down with assumed ease on a sheepskin. Nobody paid any attention to them, except the girl in front of the fire, who said to Teresa, "Do you happen to have any proper nail clippers in your bag?"

"Sorry," Teresa smiled, "Haven't I seen you somewhere before?" She knelt down beside the girl for a closer look.

"It's more than possible," the girl said. "Excuse me." Just as she was, in bare feet, she moved away to one of the young men, and Teresa sighed. Now she knew where she'd seen the girl before – on the gossip page of an evening newspaper at the opening of an art exhibition two nights before. At the opening of her own exhibition.

Soon the abstracted blue-eyed man came back with their drinks, and Tom cleared his throat.

"Perhaps you could tell us approximately what you expect for the house?" he said, and Teresa thought, how rude – couldn't he have waited until later?

"We must have a long talk about that, old chap – it's a rather difficult situation. Come back tomorrow evening and have a bite with us – then we'll see." Somewhere at one end of the room someone had started to strum a guitar and their host moved in its direction, taking Teresa by the hand with him. "Come and meet Matt Taylor."

Before a week was out, Teresa's diary had been scribbled all over on the back of the cover with famous names. Every night when they returned home to their empty flat she wrote down – lest she forget to tell her sisters – the names of new celebrities, or anyhow names she had forgotten to note on previous evenings.

Mostly there was a solid core of the same people, and with these she became fairly familiar. So she informed Tom, who sometimes demurred at yet another evening at the Wilkinsons, but usually accompanied her with a sort of resigned but growing pleasure.

All they had learned about the house was that if they produced cash (which with the help of Teresa's money and an agreed bank loan, they could), the price would be tempting and most of the carpets would be thrown in. Some of the other furnishings they could buy reasonably if they wished – the things that wouldn't travel well.

It was Tom who finally found out the reason for the sale. Mr Wilkinson – whom Teresa had long since begun to call Roger – was in danger of being closed on by his bank for a larger (horrifyingly large, it seemed to Tom) sum of money. This had been guaranteed two years ago for a poet who was emigrating with his wife and six children to the United States. The poet had paid the interest for a while, but had now stopped. Somewhere on that sizeable continent, he had simply disappeared.

"Couldn't you just pay the interest?" Tom had enquired.

"I could, but that's a life sentence. I prefer to pull out while the going's good."

"Doesn't bother you at all – I mean, morally?"

"Not at all. You must consider, after all, that I didn't borrow the money. And Monaghan's talents are such that in a rational society, like Florence during the Renaissance or medieval Ireland, for instance, he would have been supported either by the state or by a rich patron. My bank now has the honour to be a rich patron of the arts – why should the whole matter cost me one wink of sleep? This house is practically all I have, old chap, and Jennifer has nothing but an occasional sale at an occasional show and her exceptionally beautiful eyes."

Jennifer, it appeared, was the girl in jeans (only half his age) whom they had seen attending to her toenails. She seldom spoke to them but they had grown not to mind.

Occasionally Tom wondered if he was helping with a criminal transaction, but his office colleagues assured him he mustn't be a fool. He was getting the house for about three-quarters of the current market value, and the value of such houses was going up and up every year. It was an investment, his colleagues kept telling him, and he began to feel more confident about it.

One evening when Teresa was fully occupied with a school of young painters in the corner, Wilkinson beckoned Tom to come out of the room with him.

Conspiratorially he led the way to the small study in the front of the house and closed the door. Tom sank into a glorious old-fashioned leather smoking chair and looked apprehensively at his host, who offered him a cigar. Over the business of lighting this, he said in a clearly worried tone, "I'm afraid a snag has cropped up, old chap." "Yes?" Tom said, even more worried.

"It's Mary-Ann, you see. Been with the family for forty years – best years of her life and so forth. She's nearly seventy now and unemployable, I should think, though she's as good a worker as ever. The plan was of course to take her with us to London, but it won't work."

"Why?" Tom said.

"Because, quite simply, she won't come. Some peasant fear of what she calls a pagan country or something. Or just plain unwillingness to undertake the bother of moving. At any rate her mind is entirely made up so there's only one thing to do. We'll have to let her go to you with the house, old chap. If you agree you can have her and the carpets and the things Teresa has taken a fancy to for the fifty thousand. Now I can't be fairer than that."

"But," Tom suddenly shouted, "we haven't bought or sold slaves on this island since the time of St Patrick!" Wilkinson's face looked pained.

"Of course you would still pay her, old fellow. Just as we do."

"How much?" asked Tom faintly.

"Ten pounds a week and two half-days and every second Sunday off."

And so it was settled. Teresa, much to his relief, seemed to regard the arrangement as perfectly natural, although he remembered how she had frequently expressed dislike of the old woman. But Teresa was hardly herself these days. She had abandoned her white lace stockings for jeans and shaggy sweaters and she seldom came in without several newly-purchased second-hand books stuffed into the shopping bag.

On the night the Wilkinsons left, Tom and Teresa went to the North Wall to see them off, in company with many of the faithful. They weren't flying because, although so much of the heavier stuff had been sent on in a sealed truck, a great deal of baggage remained, too much for flying.

They trooped aboard, dumped the baggage and stormed into the bar. Jennifer was crying and so was Teresa but most of the company were in good spirits, and arrangements for meetings in London were bandied about. When the final hooter shrilled out, there was much embracing of everybody by everybody else. Wilkinson gripped Tom's hand in a fraternal farewell.

Outside on the quay in the drizzling cold of a spring night, Teresa and Tom suddenly found themselves alone.

"Never mind," said Teresa brightly, "they'll probably be at home before us."

He opened the car door and she jumped in, and in

the small light of the dashboard Tom carefully examined her face.

"Who will?" he said.

"Well, who do you think?" she shrugged impatiently. "Everybody."

It was now Tom's turn to shrug but she didn't notice. He drove fast through the web of fine rain that had cocooned the city, and when they got back to the house it was in darkness, with only one light burning upstairs in the old woman's room.

Teresa made exasperated noises and raced two at a time up the granite steps to the door. As soon as she let herself in she switched on the two carriage lamps on either side of the door, and then ran downstairs, leaving the door open for Tom. Downstairs she stood still for a moment and listened to the house.

It was quiet, except for Tom's footsteps, and it didn't feel so much like itself as like the hated flat they would never see again. True, the grandfather clock ticked away in the lower hall – it had been a present to her from Roger – but there was something wrong. Teresa sniffed like a dog in a strange place and pushed open the living-room door, her favourite room in all this lovely house.

Darkness. No fire. And the stars of rain glinting on the dark windowpanes. What had Mary-Ann been about? Why hadn't she lit the fire as usual at five o'clock? True, with the central heating, it wasn't strictly necessary, but conviviality was hardly possible without the friendly focus of a fire. And it always had been lit. The room didn't look too bare because of the carpet, but of course it would be better when their own furniture arrived tomorrow.

She wandered down the three steps to the kitchen and it too was in darkness. She stretched out her arms to its warm functional beauty and brushed a finger against a note left under a teapot on the solid oak counter. She read: "I thought 'twould be foolish lighting the fire across in the room with only your two selves in it. There's a beef stew and an apple cake I made for ye in the slow oven. Mary-Ann."

When Tom came in, rather superior and proud and very pleased with himself, Teresa showed him the note angrily.

"She's right," Tom said, putting on the kettle for coffee. "What would we want with a fire when the heating is switched on since morning? 'Twon't be any time before we notice the saving on coal. And how did the old girl know I go for hot apple cake?"

"But you can't properly entertain without a fire – you know that."

"Never mind about that. We're not entertaining, not this evening whatever. I was going to ask the brother over but I thought better of it. Too tired after all the pullyhauling around of the last few days. God, I am tired!" He threw himself down on a Windsor chair and stretched and yawned.

"Well I'm not tired – the idea!" Teresa angrily asserted. "You'd never know who might be here any minute."

"I would know," said Tom, with the knowing grin she had never liked. "Sweet damn nobody, that's who, and that's the way I like it. The amount of crap I've listened to in the last few weeks!"

"Very well," said Teresa, angry again. "You do

exactly what you like. I shall be at home tonight and any other night to anyone who drops in. If not tonight, then certainly tomorrow – don't you remember what a night Saturday always was in this house?"

"Look, Teresa," Tom began kindly, but just then the door-bell sounded loudly.

"Now, Tom Dunne," Teresa said triumphantly and ran away to the door. She came back with bent head, scuffling marks on the tiles with the tips of her rubber-soled shoes.

"It was our next-door neighbour. Wants to know if we have everything we need."

"Very civil," Tom said. "Have some coffee."

"I don't want any, thanks. I think I'll wait."

"Come on, Teresa. First cup in our own kitchen in our own house?"

"Well ..." Smiling doubtfully, she sat down beside him and accepted the cup. "Tomorrow we'll light the fire early and get in some beer. Saturday is the biggest night of the week, remember."

"Certainly," Tom said, "certainly." Teresa, placated, smiled at him above the rim of her coffee cup.

She had a warm vision of cheerful society, of herself casual in a paint-stained smock. Tom was cheerful also, stretching out stockinged feet to the kitchen range, thinking that he liked the house after all. Much cosier than the flat. And just as quiet.

The Honda Ward

It was the middle-aged nurse this time, the one with the double chin and she shook her head regretfully. "No love," she said, "you're not due another for half an hour. You'll never feel it passing. Sister will be along to you then." She went from him with her awkward long-assed walk to the newest arrival from the recovery room and he lay cursing and writhing in his pain, possessed by it as though it were a second skin. It began in his pelvis and throbbed down into his legs (what was left of them) and then in a moment the worst phase began, the feeling of steel jaws closing over his entire body. He ground his teeth and moaned, throwing his head from side to side of the pillow and he could feel the blood trickling from his lower lip where the teeth had bitten into it. He didn't know how long it lasted; it might have been hours. When the steel jaws began to close over him again he threw pride to the four winds and howled and at this point, as though straight on cue, his sister came in carrying daffodils. She took one look at him, dropped the flowers and tapped angrily across in her high heels to the nurse in the corner.

"I insist on seeing Sister this minute!" he heard her angry voice and the nurse said calmly: "Insist away. She'll tell you no different. He's not due another injection for half an hour."

Fidelma came running over to him and kissed his burning forehead. "I'll not let that cold bitch get the better of me. Be back to you in a minute, love!"

He gave himself up to the pain then, rolling and writhing with it, letting it split him in two and watching in his mind the two bleeding parts lying together side by side in the bed. He wished the surgeon had never put his legs together again. He wished he had never been picked up from the base of the lamp-post and carried gently to the ambulance. Lying there, before anyone came except that woman who had covered him with her fur coat and then gone shivering to the phone, lying there after it happened he had no pain. It was as though his entire body had been given one of those dental injections which freeze your gum. He felt nothing, totally out of touch with his body. He hadn't tried to get up because he didn't know where his legs were. How long ago? A week? Ten days? Longer? There was all that time in Intensive Care. He must ask Fidelma when she came back. He had forgotten to ask his father last night. It might even have been something to talk about. His father tended to go on looking at him in pity, finding very little to say.

He was between the steel jaws again, thrashing his head from side to side when Fidelma came back with the black-eyed Ward Sister who always seemed to be on the point of smiling. She brushed back his hair with a cool hand and looked sharply at him, "I'll have you right as rain in two minutes, Bonzo," she said, and walked elegantly away. It was five minutes, Fidelma muttered angrily, before she came back and even then she did not carry a hypodermic syringe but two white tablets on a little dish. "Get these down you now, James and they'll see you through to the next injection," and then he let himself go and hissed SHIT at her, although she only smiled back with great sweetness at him. He downed the useless things then, closed his eyes and tried to master the pain for Fidelma's sake. He imagined himself floating down a river with fire on either side of him. burning oil slicks maybe, although what would they be doing on a river? If he held his body tightly together the flames might not reach him. After what seemed a long time he floated free of the flames and there were tall yellow irises instead and cool river weeds on every side of him. He opened his eyes and saw Fidelma was crying a bit.

"I'm OK Fiddle, swear it. Never knew the little white buggers to work before."

"Great!" she said, smiling at him, her eyes dry in a moment. She started to arrange the daffodils in a vase on the window sill and she threw some dead ones in a bucket before sitting down again.

"All the gang were asking for you, Jim," she said. "They'll be in to see you tonight – well some of them." "What day is it?"

"Friday."

"Oh God, Friday! Then it's two weeks since …"

"Yes!"

"I still have two legs, did you know that?"

"Did I know? Jesus, didn't we stay up all night, Dad and I! The first word that came over the phone was that you'd probably lose the left one, and Dad was wracked with tears the same as me before they phoned again. Mr Ryan had been called in out of his bed and saved the left one. Then we didn't care anymore. Dad made whiskey punch for the pair of us and we went to bed."

"Punch? Dad?"

"There you are now, he did. He'll be in to see you this afternoon as well. Early he says, and the lads will come later. I have to go now or I'll miss my French class."

When his father came he was shyly pleased to see the improvement and Jim didn't tell him that the injection was only ten minutes old. Some neighbour had given his old man a holy medal for poor Jim to wear around his neck and he didn't reject it out of hand. Reaching out, he put it beside the fruit on his locker and he could see the effort it took his father to refrain from repeating that the medal was to be worn around the neck on the cord provided.

"How's the form anyway?" his father repeated. He had a habit of repeating everything.

"Great, Dad," he said. "Tell me about the bike."

"She's not as bad as you might think. I've got her home now, of course, and now that you're a bit better I'll have the heart to check her carefully over the weekend. The front fork is distorted, of course, and the tyre is in ribbons and the rim is so far out of true that it will probably mean a new wheel, but we'll get over that. By the time you come home, Jim, I'll probably have her in good order again." Even as the father spoke, he felt he was being treacherous to his daughter who had strongly argued forgetting about the bike, selling it for scrap rather, and lodging the proceeds to James's savings account. He felt it was too early yet to make such a sweeping decision on his son's behalf.

His limited store of small talk was almost exhausted when the first of the Honda crowd came spilling into the ward. Each of them pulled off his helmet and laid it down carefully along by the wall before turning to greet Jim. The father took his leave.

"How's it going? How's the fella then?"

There were five of them in bikers' boots and they were bursting with health and red-cheeked from the cold outside. They all seemed taller than he remembered and they made him feel nervous, even defenceless. If in one of their scufflings they fell on his bed and knocked over the cage which protected his legs who knows what might happen? He looked up at the white mountain the cage made in front of him and he knew it was kept in place by tightly tucked bedclothes and that he was being neurotic to feel threatened. Yet he listened to the shop talk of school and sport and wild weekends as though he were an outsider and older and all this had nothing to do with him and never would have again. Two of them squatted on the floor, the rest had borrowed chairs and sat happily around him. Nobody, he was thankful to note, tried to sit on his bed.

"Sparky is brilliant these last few practices," Harding was saying. "Macker is trying him out for wing three-quarter. He might make the final in Lansdowne if he keeps it up."

"Not a chance!" Fanning said. "Too lazy, too fond of the booze and the birdies. It'll be Kennedy again like last year."

"The knee is not right yet," Fahey reminded them. "Kennedy has to keep it quiet for a while yet."

"He's started training again," Brown said. "Saw him jogging past the house this morning."

As they talked, they casually devoured his apples, his grapes and his chocolates and they were just about to pass around his fags when he had to stop them.

"You'll be thrown out of here if you light up fellas," he said. "Take them away if you want to – I've no taste for them since it happened."

Fanning winked and pocketed the fags and then they began to talk about school. Feeler, the History master, was going to be posted to another Jesuit house – in Siberia most likely. Brown leered and they all guffawed knowingly.

Stop it, he said, stop it for fuck's sake. But no words came out of his dry lips. The closing steel teeth of pain had started up again. Go away, he said to his mates. Go away. But they went on. Gossip, news, gags he had to hear about. Fighting the pain, he found himself thinking about his mother for the first time in a while, wishing she could come through that door. She had been tall, even gangly and leggy like an overgrown schoolgirl and she had hardly ever stopped talking. Except when you were sick, that is. Then she had always known what to do, how to calm you, exactly what food to bring up and even what to say to raise a laugh and make you forget your miseries. She had thickly fringed grey eyes whose expression he could no longer recall and very white teeth but also a nose that looked like a boxer's and would never cause anybody to describe her as pretty. Yet she was dark and glossy and her perfume used to hang around after she was gone. She was gone a long time now – two years? He thought he was fifteen when she died and Fidelma thirteen. Fidelma was a bit like her to look at, except she had a nicer nose and Fidelma too could sometimes know exactly what you were thinking and do the right thing. Like today. He remembered fellows in school giving out about their old dears and not knowing what they were talking about. He wished she could have walked in through the door today instead of Fidelma. Would she have said something to make him laugh instead of cry? The steel jaws gripped him again and he beat his head from side to side and Fanning's big voice grated into his ear:

"Are you OK Lowry? Look we better be going, old son. Get you the nursing bird on the way out, OK?"

"See ya, Lowr," he heard one after another of their voices saying and then he heard the trampling of their boots and the rattle of their helmets as they took them up from the corner inside the door and clattered away down the corridor.

Sometimes he didn't even try to stop the tears dripping down his face and this was one of those times. He looked at his watch and knew he would have to wait fifteen minutes for another injection. Afraid of making him a junkie, they were. They were carefully rationing out the only thing that was any good to him, morphine. This time it might be administered by Beckett again. Nurse Beckett was from the North and she had told him her name was Caroline. She was a student nurse, really, not yet qualified and she wasn't much older than he was himself. He would surprise her by not moaning like a dog and thrashing about but facing the pain head on and besting it. His tears had dried on his face and there was five minutes to go.

"My aren't we the brave wee lad today and no mistake!" Caroline said, coming on him unawares. "How are we then?"

"Lousy, thank you," he grinned up at her.

"I'll have to give you another bed bath so," she said archly, and he found himself blushing which annoyed him so much that he forgot the pain. He had found it odd, in the beginning, during his rare moments of lucidity to find himself being intimately yet impersonally touched by women young and old in the ordinary course of their day's work. They might have been polishing furniture for all it mattered to them he often thought. It didn't matter even when he had to urinate into a tube for them and let them unstrap the bag from the bed and carry it away to be emptied. It didn't matter now that he had graduated to a bottle which had to be requested each time. But today when Caroline exposed his left buttock for the injection he coloured slightly and wondered if it was accidental that her little finger brushed his limp penis as she was settling back the bedclothes.

"Stay awhile and talk to me," he said to her.

"Is it hanged, drawn and quartered you'd have me James?" she murmured. "There's a wee crabbed bitch out there waiting to jump on me, so there is and I'll not give her reason. Mebbe tomorrow, though. " She winked at him and went bouncing off on her flat heels, pink-cheeked and grinning, a few curls of brown hair ringing her cap at the back as he looked after her. Nineteen, twenty? Seventeen like himself? Tomorrow he'd ask her.

After his meal the last person he ever expected to see coming through the door to visit him was Feeler, but it couldn't possibly have been anybody else, he thought, even allowing for the spaced state he was in. Nobody but Feeler had that sharp-nosed country look under the thatch of sandy hair, the crooked teeth white as a hound's, the small limp womanish hands that seemed as though they ought to belong to somebody else. Feeler settled himself comfortably in the only armchair after a damp handshake.

"How's the boy?" he asked. He had a midland accent, soft and flat, and the big froggy pale-blue eyes rested sympathetically on the patient.

"Fine, sir."

"Have you any pain still?"

"Usually, yes. But they've fixed me up for the time being with an injection."

"The wonders of science," Feeler smiled. "The wind outside would skin a weasel, so you may as well enjoy the bed while you can. " So far so clichéd, the boy thought. But something about the confident way this man filled the chair and looked across at him under the sandy fuzz suggested that he would not go away without saying something that you could remember.

"You won't thank me for it, but I've brought you a bit of work, Jim. " He reached down into his briefcase, took out a few pages and laid them on the tray in front of

James. "Work away on these whenever you can and send the finished job into me by one of the visiting fellows. You'll be well back on your feet before the exams and you won't want to be left behind by the rest of them. After all, it wasn't your brain suffered in the smash, was it?"

"Sometimes I'm not so sure," the boy muttered, a vague feeling of animosity suddenly coming like a cold wind between them. He didn't want to work in bed. Nobody else had suggested he should. And Feeler after all was on his way out.

"They tell me you'll be leaving us soon Sir?"

"True enough," Feeler said indifferently, "but one way or another that needn't bother you. I'm here until the end of the summer term and I see no reason why we shouldn't try to get you through your bloody exams."

"Thanks, Sir, I'll do what I can with the questions, but my writing is a bit worse than usual since it happened. I hope it won't drive you mad."

"Don't bother your head about that. My own handwriting gets more and more like the path home of a drunken spider. I'll manage yours fine. Anything bothering you?" Again the look was sharp under the sandy hair, the almost white eyebrows. The boy didn't really understand why he wanted suddenly to talk to this odd man.

"Could you – could you tell them to keep the Chaplain out of my way, Sir? I haven't the guts to do it myself and they might listen to you. I couldn't really discuss it with my father. He left in this to me," and the patient indicated the medal on the table beside him.

"Maybe I'll find a good home for that," Feeler said,

scooping it into his pocket and then fixing on the boy his bland-eyed country-cute look he asked:

"What s the holy man done to you, James, to incur your displeasure?"

"Oh nothing much, really, it's just that ... " He looked down frowning at the blue bedspread, selecting his words carefully. "It's just that he was there looming over me – he's a big heavy man – when I was carted in, not knowing properly where I was and he kept nagging at me to make a good confession. He'd been sitting there when the two surgeons were talking about me, after I'd been given the injection. For a long time it took no effect because the Chaplain leaned over and said that the doctors as a general rule did a good job on fellows like me but of course nothing was certain and it was his duty as God's minister to be here ready and willing to give me absolution of my sins if only I'd make a good confession before being carried in to the operating theatre. Some people dying on the side of the road never got the chance and I was one of the lucky ones. A good act of contrition now after I'd confessed my sins would put me right with God if it so happened He wanted to call me this very day, did I understand?"

"Jesus wept!" exploded Feeler. "He said that to you and you flat on your back waiting to go in to the theatre?"

"Yes he did. Sir."

"And he frightened you into confessing?"

"No." Jim was smiling now. "But he did, I suppose, frighten me. They had to come back and give me another injection and they seemed surprised that I hadn't gone drowsy. After that I don't remember too much except the

128

anaesthetist telling me to count backwards from ten and before I'd finished I was back in bed somewhere else, in Intensive Care as it turned out, and it was over."

"Have you seen the man since?"

"No, but Lent will soon be starting I hear, and it struck me he might try again. I'd rather not see him anymore."

"No bloody wonder. I can promise you you won't. Of course it might be regarded as none of my business but you've no mother and I'm going to speak to the old Matron on my way out. The man should be packed away sharpish out of here before he can do any more harm. Leave it to me, Jim."

"Thanks, Sir. I could make a bit of headway with the questions if I had my textbooks in the locker here. I'll ask Fidelma to bring them in."

"No need, fella." Feeler leaned in to the briefcase again and then put the textbooks on the bedside table. "Fire away with these, maybe early in the mornings next week, if you can sit up a bit by then. See how you get on. I'll be in to see you again anyway. If you're not able for the whole effort, don't worry – I'll be talking to you about it again. Keep the old heart up now!"

Feeler made a last swoop into the briefcase and hauled out two packets of potato crisps, ten fags and a couple of Mars bars before he fastened it up and was gone, leaving the patient smiling in the direction of the door.

Half an hour later, in the valley time between tea and the bulk of evening visitors, he stared in disbelief at the large familiar priest bearing down on him from that same door.

This time the man was dressed in a black polo-neck sweater and anorak and he was rubbing his huge hands to indicate the cold of outdoors.

"Lucky man to be where you are tonight, James. 'Twould freeze the marrow of your bones out there. How are you?"

Recoiling with every functioning muscle in his body, the boy stared at the closely shaved pink face, the grizzled hair cut close and bristling, the round black-rimmed glasses whose dazzle from the bedside lamp fortunately hid the eyes. Trapped, all he could think of doing was to close his eyes and lie there as though dead. The pain which had been dormant started to pulse through him again.

"Come on Jimmy, you were bright enough when I came in. God is good, and believe me there's a world of difference between the bright lad I saw and I coming through that door and the poor fellow carted in off the road in bits two weeks ago. God has been very good to you Jimmy, and don't you forget it."

Still he kept his eyes firmly shut, willing himself elsewhere, willing the loathsome hearty voice to go away. He willed it so hard that he half-thought God had indeed been very good and struck the man dumb to grant the sinner James this blessed silence. Furthermore he had not been touched, but then, it would have been quite difficult to touch him. He had snatched his hands instinctively under the bed-clothes on the priest's arrival and he lay there tense and motionless until he felt the heavy hand on his forehead. The words of the blessing had hardly ended when he opened his eyes and said deliberately "Fuck off, Father."

The priest pretended not to hear and sat heavily down by the bedside. Trembling after his effort, the boy closed his eyes again, pain strumming now in every part of his body. He tried to remember *So all day long the noise of battle rolled among the mountains by the winter sea* and when it failed there was *Ride a cock horse to Banbury Cross* and *How many miles to Babylon* and anything to keep the loathsome noise away, but it kept thickly breaking through.

God was merciful but he did expect a little in return. Remember the healing of the ten lepers. His sense of Divine Justice was outraged when only one came back to give thanks. His patience was not infinite and if people who had been granted great favours didn't turn to Him (worse, if they turned away from Him) then God would not be mocked.

Again, as on the day when James had been carried in on a stretcher to this hospital, absolution was now offered to him (God was merciful too remember, ever ready to forgive if only His creature would confess his sins and be sorry for them). He James, to whom God had been so good, had not only refused initially to make his peace with Him, but had actually schemed to try to ensure that the sacramental grace of a good confession would not be offered to him again.

In a sudden burst of decision the boy leaned painfully up and rang the bell behind his head several times, still without looking at the priest. The big man got to his feet and made a gesture of blessing just as a young student nurse came through from the main ward, exchanged a joke with her and went rambling away to the rest of the patients in the Honda ward.

"I think I'm going to be sick," he said to Nurse Beckett.

She fetched him the small plastic kidney-shaped dish and held him while he filled it. She wiped his mouth as he lay back quivering. She smiled at him, then poured him a glass of the glucose drink, which she gave him with two white pills.

"Here Jim," she said. "Put back a little of the liquid you lost that time. You'll feel the better of it, so you will."

He did too. He felt ready to hold her to her promise of talking to him even if it was not tomorrow yet. The pain gradually receded again.

"Do you never get browned off with all the horrible whining sick people you have to deal with?" he asked her and she shook her head with great energy.

"Never. Some of the well ones are a deal worse, I can tell you, naming no names." She winked and then he knew she meant the chaplain and a great grin spread all over his face. "There's them around the place I'd give the bum's rush to if I'd any say in it so I would, but I haven't. Three years to go or maybe four if I do my midwifery and then I'm away to Canada like the devil was at my heels, same as my sister. Alberta, Canada here I come, fast as I can make it!"

She giggled and hooked the straps of imaginary dungarees with her thumbs.

"What will you do there, Caroline?" She'd never

actually told him that he could use her name but she obviously didn't mind.

"Work in one of the rich private clinics probably. That's where you make the bread AND meet mining millionaires. Mebbe even private nursing in big houses if I take the notion."

"I don't think there's too much private nursing in people's homes anywhere in the world now," he said. "But why not the States?"

"My sister says Canada is nicer and it's easier to get to know people. Sure I'm mebbe kidding about the millionaires. But I like people to be friendly and I love plenty of money in my pocket, not that I know too much about it. What will you do?"

"Haven't a clue. Can't see much beyond my Leaving if I ever get it after this. You need about forty points to have any choice of faculties in college."

"You could mebbe do a bit of work in bed instead of gosthering, couldn't you?"

"I mean to," he said.

"Tell you what," she said suddenly, "I'll take you for a wee walk – see some of the other star acts before the visitors come. Be back in a wink."

She returned with a wheelchair, and the pain as she helped him into it nearly made him faint but he held on.

"When the stitches are out, Jim, it will be better. The physiotherapist will make your joints work properly again and you'll be right as rain. Easy now."

She whirled him through onto the main part of the Honda ward of which he had seen only one small corner through his door. He was supposed to be a semi-private patient but nobody had come to replace the fellow who had gone home from his room. Out here there were twelve patients round about his own age, some of them sitting up reading copies of *Bike*, several with legs strung up and suspended from a pulley at the end of the bed, some with bandaged heads or arms, some lying flat with spinal injuries and all cheerfully, it seemed, resigned to their lot. The fellow they paused beside offered him a cigarette and Nurse Beckett turned her back obligingly, saying she would come and fetch him later on. The fellow's name was Dave and he had a broken pelvis and two broken wrists. His fingers emerging from the plaster were bluish but he could hold the biking magazine all right.

"Look at this three-cylinder job-isn't she a beaut? They say she's got a vicious power band but that the frame and brakes are the best yet."

"She's all that. A rich guy in school was given one the same last year by his old man. Hasn't come off her yet!" Dave grinned with his white chipped teeth.

"Give him time, mate. What was your problem anyhow?"

"Gave a guy a lift home from school and he didn't know how to go with her around a corner. Huge heavy boots. Things went completely out of control and I hit a lamp-post."

"What about the passenger?"

"Not a scratch on him, and he hadn't even got a helmet. "

"The way the cookie crumbles," Dave said indifferently.

"What about yourself?"

"Got a better run for my money than that," he grinned amiably. "Asking for it you might say. Seven or eight pints in me one Saturday night and I was coming home at a fair old wallop on the Bray road. That's all I can remember. The buzz of going well. Seems I encountered a Merc somewhere around the Kilcroney crossroads. Damaged her pretty paint quite a bit. I'm glad to say, but of course the driver wasn't scratched. They seldom are."

Jim nodded silently, impressed by the seven or eight pints bit. "Will you take her out again?"

"You kidding? Can't wait to get out of here and back on to her again. Haven't been without wheels since I was fourteen and you can bet your shirt I won't be going back to a push-bike at seventeen. Not a chance!" He was, he said, an apprentice electrician and he was saving up for a big job when he was out of his time. "You quitting?" he said to Jim then, who shrugged.

"Hard to say. There'll be a bit of pressure from home. Don't know how I'll feel about it when the pain stops and I can walk again."

"You'll feel fine about it."

"Expect so." Jim wished Beckett would come back and take him away as the first of the helmeteers arrived in a blast of sound. The steel teeth had started to close again around his thighs and he knew his face had gone white as he dug his nails into the palms of his hands. Dave was quick to notice his condition despite the fact that two of the visitors were for him.

"Hey," he said to one of them, "put this guy back in Millionaires' Row and make a bit of room for yourselves. See ya, Jim."

"See ya." The fellow who had wheeled him in looked down concerned at him.

"You OK?"

"Sure. Give that bell a buzz before you go, could you?"

"Will do." The big freckled redhead ambled off in his biking boots, and Jim could hear the guffaws of laughter coming in from there and see the drifts of smoke curling upwards. It seemed like half an hour before Beckett came running in to him, fixing a pin in her cap and full of apologies.

"Hold on there Jim till I get Nurse Keogh to give me a hand. Then we won't hurt you."

The two nurses seemed to flip him deftly out of the wheelchair and on to his bed where he lay back quivering.

"Mebbe we rushed you a bit, Jim," Beckett said. "Next week you'll be better able for this, won't he Nurse?"

"Sure," Nurse Keogh said, patting his shoulder before she hurried off.

"A cup of coffee just for this once," Beckett said.

"Love one, Caroline," he managed to smile at her and that was what helped him over the next hour of visitors. Last of all his father came, bearing a pink primula in a pot from the neighbour who had sent him the holy medal.

"Mrs Fahey says she's having a mass said for you on Thursday," his father told him. "Isn't that very good of her? And she says she'll ask Fr O'Dowd who's the Chaplain here to keep a special eye on you. He's a second cousin of her husband's. She says to tell you that she's sorry the arthritis keeps her from visiting you herself."

"Dad will you do something for me? Thank Mrs

Fahey for her kindness and for the plant but tell her to keep the second cousin of her husband's as far away from me as possible – if she can."

"How could I bring a nice neighbour an extraordinary message like that? What would your poor mother say if she could only hear you?"

"She'd understand – Christ I could talk to her," Jim burst out, already regretting it. "Sorry Dad, forgive me, but I do not want to see the hospital Chaplain anywhere near this bed ever again. If he comes I won't speak to him, any more than I did today. That's all."

His father looked baffled and anxious and quite obviously hadn't an idea how to handle it.

"You see Dad, I'm just not on the same wavelength as Father O'Dowd and the thing is you feel *trapped* in bed by somebody like that who can just walk in and out as he pleases, invading you. I'm sorry if this worries you but you can forget what I asked you anyway. I'll deal with it myself. Or with a little help from my friends," he grinned in further apology.

"I simply don't understand you, James," his father said. "Maybe it's all those drugs have you upset."

"Maybe that's it. Thanks for coming in. Dad, and thank Mrs Fahey for the lovely plant and tell her not to trouble herself about the Chaplain – because we see him all the time, OK?"

"That sounds fair enough," his father said, though it was obvious that he was far from satisfied. "How's the form today otherwise?"

"Great. I was up for the first time today in a wheelchair – how about that?"

"Splendid, son. Fidelma has a maths grind tonight and can't come, but she'll be delighted when I tell her."

And I had a visit from Father Duncan our history teacher. He brought in some work and he's going to make sure I don't become a layabout in here."

"I see," said his father, doubtful again. "Did you know Father Duncan is leaving at the end of next term?"

"Oh yes – more's the pity. He's a great teacher."

"I'm sure he is," said his father. "One has doubts about his suitability all the same."

"All gossip," Jim said firmly and he looked kindly at his father for the first time. He felt a great deal older than the grey-haired man looked and he felt that eventually he would be able to spare him an amount of worry about things the man would never be able to understand.

Summer in London

It had been Eleanor's idea and she had described this orgy in Harrods very well. Her mother had taken her there after the exams on her annual shopping spree in London last year. Eleanor had described the breeze billowing through white tulle curtains, the starched tablecloths, the pianist playing Palm Court music with liberal use of the soft pedal, the air of slothful luxury in the middle of London on an ordinary Tuesday afternoon.

But no words her friends remembered could have done justice to the flower-filled altar itself. They had clutched one another and fallen around laughing at the looped white linen, the trailing Victorian garlands of leaves, the fresh flowers which garnished the table on which were spread out hundreds of sugar confections. There were meringues of every colour and shape, cherry cakes and chocolate cakes and Battenburg cakes, there were fluffy dark devil's food cakes with sugar violets on top and strawberry flans stiff with cream and of course there were chocolate éclairs and every imaginable kind of bun. Neither Una nor Catherine could believe that all you had to do once a waitress had found you a table was take one or two plates from it and go off to collect your own loot. Once the £5 had been paid in advance (only £3.75 last year, Eleanor had said) you could pick and choose as you might in your own flower garden. There were the be-frilled waitresses and boys in white coats to help you to things which needed cutting such as large cartwheels of Black Forest cherry cake in kirsch and gateaux which looked like something which might have been served to Marie Antoinette in the Petit Trianon. Catherine giggled nervously as she remembered the rigidity of the diet she had followed before deciding to come to London on a summer job.

"Don't think about it," Eleanor kindly advised, "just enjoy it. We won't come again."

"Not if we are to save £150 each in six weeks and stay alive at the same time," Una said, grimly.

"Relax," Eleanor said. She had a self-indulgent mother who encouraged the celebration of practically everything. It was easy for her. "I'm not taking a penny from either of you," Eleanor smiled. "This is just something I want to treat us all to. So just let's be hogs and enjoy it or I'll wish I hadn't been such a fool."

Giggling as though they were back at school again, they heaped up their plates as the pianist put his soft-pedal foot down again and played "You Will Remember Vienna." Back at their table they eyed one another's plates and giggled again. White curtains puffed out behind them like bridal veils.

"Two cream horns seems a bit ambitious," Una said.

"Don't worry, there won't be a single crumb left," said Eleanor. But there was more. There was a whole cream horn left on her plate when she finally admitted

140

defeat. Una had eaten her way through everything, however (although she kept saying that what she would really like was a heap of raw grated carrot), and Catherine had left half an éclair. Eleanor poured more tea for them all and the pianist tinkled on. "I keep wondering why anybody comes alone to a place like this," Eleanor said softly at last, nodding towards a huge lady in a pink straw hat whose face was red from effort.

"She's come alone every Friday for fifteen years since her best friend who was at school with her died," invented Catherine. "They lived in Croyden and always came by train to shop at the Food Hall every Friday. Afternoon tea up here was their little treat for the week. Her friend was called Rose and she is Ivy."

"I think it's obscene," Una shuddered. "They all look so greedy. Every time more cakes are carried in some of them go up again. That little thin man (how does he do it?) with the panama hat and the buttonhole – he's up and down like a Jack-in-the-box."

"I think he's sweet," said Eleanor. "He only goes up to look. Mostly he doesn't take anything else."

"I suppose it keeps them out of the pubs, " Una decided at last. "That's about all you can say in its favour. All that money for junk food!"

"Saying that is hardly a polite response to an invitation that I for one think is fun and am thoroughly enjoying. I'll always remember the way we spent our first afternoon together in London." Catherine was nothing if not mannerly. They hadn't in fact known one another very well in college – not well enough for that sort of frankness anyhow. It had simply happened that they had discovered they were all going to London for the same reason and might as well keep in touch. Catherine ended her civil speech by smiling happily at Eleanor who in turn looked relieved.

"It was different when I came with Mother last year. She remembered it from the fifties, you see, when she and my father chose London for their honeymoon. She kept telling me about the string orchestra which used to play and the starched table napkins and the fifty different kinds of scone alone you could choose from and the special flowery dresses all the women wore. It cost £1 then, I think, and my father said he could live here. Which didn't surprise me to hear because Mother admitted she wooed him with Bewley's coffee and chocolate biscuits in Ranelagh."

"He wouldn't live long on this diet, " Una stuck sourly to her guns, "nor deserve to. Are you all ready?"

"He's alive and well thank you and devoted at other times of the day to yoghurt and steak and coleslaw," said Eleanor, with a broad smile.

In a way, it was like pulling themselves out of a fairy tale but they got their belongings together at last and surfaced. The Barcarolle from "The Tales of Hoffman" followed them softly out into the furniture department. Catherine sat down suddenly on one of the creaking wicker chairs.

"I think I'm going to be sick," she said, and looked it.

"I know where the loo is – quick!" said Eleanor and led the way. Catherine could unfortunately be heard being sick and she looked surprised when she emerged from the lavatory.

They didn't see one another again for a week, and then only because Eleanor phoned the other two. She was working as a chambermaid in a central London hotel called "The Sir Roger" because Addison was reputed to have stayed there for several years.

It was now long past its prime except for the hall which still looked like the entrance to a comfortable country house. The dining-room and the room still marked "Drawing Room" had brightly polished brasses and a lot of old mahogany. Several castor oil plants had somehow survived since the days when they were last fashionable and now, in vogue again, they were a sumptuous contrast to the plastic flower arrangements of more modern and more expensive hotels. But as you progressed lower down or higher up into the house the place degenerated into the ruin it really was. Untreated dry rot had mushrooms sprouting evilly all over the larders and kitchens. The sound of rats scampering and foraging at night frequently frightened away new male staff who were expected to sleep tumbled together in strange cell-like places reeking of damp. Upstairs the damp from missing slates and un-cleaned gutters made the old wallpaper billow and ooze, the paint crumble away.

The worst bedrooms of all were under the roof of the house where the female staff slept five or six to a room. In heavy rain you had to catch the drips in plastic buckets and if you forgot to empty them in time the floods met you on your way up to bed. The manager only worried when the water seeped down into the guest rooms on the fourth floor.

Eleanor had been adaptable since childhood and kept telling herself she was lucky to have a job in the very heart of London. The rest of the housemaids and chambermaids were all right to work with if not very comfortable to sleep with, and the only thing she found intolerable was the heat of the linen room where she spent most of every day. She had to collect changes of linen there, put away the stuff just back from the laundry and do the ironing. The housekeeper was particular about the appearance of the shelves in case the manager should ever choose to look in but she wasn't particular about changing the linen after one-night stays. Part of Eleanor's job was to iron used sheets so that they looked new when put back on the beds. After one night's use, however, they were only topped and tailed for the next guest, and ironed for the third. As soon as they began to be noticeably unfresh, however, Eleanor had to make sure they went to be laundered. She began to know the look of guests whose linen would not survive to be used again and it amused her (however clean they might look) to be proved right.

It was one of the few amusements of her job. The heat in the linen room was so overpowering (because it was directly over the main boiler) that she often had to remove her dress and work in bra and knickers with sweat pouring from her. Mrs Ledmore was furious the first time she discovered the new chambermaid thus divested but she stopped complaining the day Eleanor passed out with the heat and had to be revived with cold face cloths and an extravagant sip of brandy.

The three girls met next time in the coffee bar of the National Gallery one pouring wet afternoon in July. Eleanor was crying to the dismay of the others and they wondered what had happened to her determined cheerfulness of just a week ago. Catherine tried to make her laugh by dumping on her plate a tiny thing like a grass snake. She said she had tended it from a seedling and looked after it like a mother.

"What is it?" Eleanor managed to ask, blowing her nose and then quickly putting away her handkerchief.

"It's going to be a courgette," said Catherine, "or rather if I'd not uprooted it, that's what it would be. All its family are courgettes." She worked for a market gardener in Kent and made fifty pounds a week. By living in a hostel she might save twenty pounds a week, or even more.

Una asked bluntly what was wrong with Eleanor. Crying never solved anything. Catherine tried to hush her, but it was too late. "Kevin is here in London, " Eleanor said at last. "He came to see me yesterday at the hotel." Tears began to pour down her face again but no sound came.

"I know exactly what's wrong with you," Una said. "He's upset you by raising objections. Your mind was made up, and now it isn't."

"Exactly," Eleanor agreed, and took out her handkerchief again. This time she dried her face and no more tears came but she drew in a couple of very deep breaths. "He says he doesn't want me to do it. Says if I do it the odds are I may never have another child – this happens, he says – and anyhow, it's ours, not just mine. I should see it, he says, and so should he, and then we should decide if we can go through with adoption."

"Is he staying in London?" Una wanted to know.

"Just for two days on his way to Holland. He'll be working there until October."

"Easy for him to be sentimental, isn't it?" Una said savagely. "His baby for God's sake! Why don't you give it to him now and let him carry it the rest of the way?"

They all laughed. Eleanor drank a glass of milk and decided to be cheerful again. "I half agree with him, you know. Maybe I never will have another child. Maybe it would have been brilliant and beautiful. James Stephens was a bastard and so was Sarah Bernhardt. You just have to do nothing once the thing starts, and then you have a baby. You don't have to say, 'Today I'll make its legs and tomorrow its brains.' You have to do nothing but eat properly and stay sane and then in nine months you have a baby that's like no other in the world and that's yours for ever and his. Always biologically yours and his whoever may rear it."

"Stop it, stop it!" Una said. "All the reasons for which you came to London are still valid. You don't *want* a baby, you never asked for one, and your life will be ruined if you go ahead. Quite simply you were a careless fool like everybody else and you're pregnant. Happily it's reversible."

Catherine had been playing with the courgette. "I see what she means, though. You can't help thinking along those lines when you work in my job. Growth itself is a fascination. Especially the private growth in your own body which takes other people so long to notice."

"Not all that long," said Una grimly. "Do nothing and they'll notice soon enough. And then at that stage the whole business is grisly and I can understand why nurses hate it. But none of that need happen in our cases. I've already made arrangements (God be good to you Marie

146

Stopes!) for July 20th. I'd thought both of you would have done the same by now."

"I have," Eleanor said quickly, "July 28th is my date. It's just that I'm not sure any more."

"Nor am I," Catherine said, "even although I was delighted last week when I got the result of the examination and the signatures of the two doctors. I was absolutely certain then that I was doing the only sensible thing in the circumstances. But that was last week ..." Her voice trailed off on a sigh.

Una shook her head in exasperation. "I simply don't believe what I'm hearing. How would you *both* have felt if the doctors had refused to refer you and you were stuck? Have you the remotest idea of what rearing a child on your own means? My sister ..."

"Please," said Eleanor, "we know all the arguments. It's just that I'm no longer sure I want to do it."

"My mother, for instance," said Catherine, "would probably love to have a child running around the house again."

"I wouldn't bank on it," Una said grimly. "Empty nest syndrome is all very well at one level. At another the woman wouldn't be human if she wasn't actually glad that all the donkey-work was over. Beginning all over again in late middle age because your daughter has been an imbecile wouldn't be everybody's cup of tea and maybe not your mother's. You didn't tell her anyway."

"Only because I knew her views on abortion. The bishops have told her what to think and she takes their word for it. Murder!"

"A few pregnant bishops would alter everything in a

remarkably short time. Roll on the ordination of women, I say."

It was still raining after tea so they wandered around the Flemish rooms which seemed to be full of pregnant women, on the walls or looking at them. During a break in the rain they all walked to Oxford Street with Catherine who wanted to buy a blurry print dress full enough to allow for growth while she saved her money and suitable in design for being glimpsed amid the apple trees. Catherine was inclined to be romantic.

She smiled to herself over this as she clutched the parcel from Selfridges on her way back by underground to her village. She had to get a bus when the line petered out at last among the straggling fields and on the bus she felt queasy. To distract her mind she thought of the baby after seven weeks growth, trying to remember the photographs she had seen as a twelve-year-old gaining instruction. Somewhere inside that weird shape were the genes and chromosomes which would give it male or female sex, brown eyes or blue, fine dark hair like her own or rough brown curly hair like Brendan's, even perhaps a way of clearing its throat like her father's, or a tendency to walk with toes turned in like her mother's. She wondered if anything could change a pre-ordained order at this stage, as more or less light could change the contours of a plant. She had lulled herself to such a state of amused calm that she wasn't sick this time and the sight of Brendan waiting in the dusk at the bus stop was merely a miracle she had half expected. They had parted on bad terms and he had called her irresponsible and careless. Now he was the old affectionate joking Brendan once again who had, it seemed found a job not too far away, in the hop fields. He assumed she'd had the abortion already and hoped she would share a room with him over a little pub. She would, and suddenly she felt cheerful for the first time in many weeks. She'd made up her mind. No point in complicating everything by being stupidly stubborn at this stage. She'd phone Una tomorrow.

Una had the softest job of the three, with her own Laura Ashley-style bedroom at the back of a mews house off Kensington High Street. When she looked out from her window she could see past the spire of St Mary Abbot's along the green sward of Kensington Gardens to the fountains. Because of the trees the traffic sounds were muffled. In the mornings she took the children out walking, and after lunch she gave pre-school lessons to the older child while the younger one was having his nap. Una disliked children on the whole but found Emma and Andrew bearable. Their doctor parents had trained them to be amiable with a variety of strangers who had cared for them since birth.

Una was responsible for preparing a simple lunch for herself and the children but a woman who came in the afternoons cooked dinner, usually a good one. When the parents were staying in the city Una had to see the children to bed and was supposed to read to them. But in fact the cook, who had grandchildren of her own, often did that and Una escaped to the park or out for a drink with the Arab student she had met at a concert in the Albert Hall. She was punctilious about being back in time to let Mrs Markham home at her usual time and about never leaving the children alone.

Sometimes the evenings were long. When the light lingered and she grew tired of her few tapes and bored (as she'd always been) by television, she sometimes went in to check that the children were all right and at such times their sleeping faces seemed to her defenceless and even beautiful. Andrew's anyway. Once, with the bathroom windows wide open, she stripped off all her clothes and examined her body in the filtered green light from the park. It was still, as it had always been, lean, long-waisted and small-breasted with ribs showing and the hip bones a bit spiky. He hadn't liked them. Said he preferred the Juno type but for some reason Junos were a bit thin (ha ha) on the ground this year. It was the thirties-style clothes that had everyone slimmed down to the bone. His last lady before leaving home had been a pretty cow, however, lush where biologically necessary. Una said he wasn't exactly her type either. She preferred a little more brains, less brawn, and a lot more energy. The jokes were known by both to be rather more than half serious. There was no question of a love affair. Simply both had other plans which came to nothing and they had somehow been thrown together that term in college. Sometimes they made one another laugh and there had never been any question of telling him she was pregnant. That would have been the biggest joke of all.

What worried her about having the abortion was a trivial thing really. After a long enjoyable shower, she examined her body again in the green light. What worried her was giving it voluntarily over for storming. She knew that afterwards it felt like no more than a heavy period. That's all it was really. Nothing. Accidental fertilisation of an egg, unplanned multiplication of little cells, a bit more than the womb lining to shed at the end of six weeks or so. That was all. Sometimes it happened naturally and then people got upset if they happened to be married and happened to want a child. The actual abortion thing itself was expensive and a nuisance and she didn't like the thought of surrendering herself for money to other people, blindly taking their skills for granted because that was all one could do. She thought it more than likely she'd feel exactly the same about a birth. That was a sort of surrender too and you were prepared by clinical hands as for an operation, the way her sister had been.

She got angry all over again when she remembered the stupid way it happened: carelessness about going in time for another prescription. A few days without pills and he had to take her to a party, to a place she'd never been before, near Celbridge where he lived. He knew his way well around the house and eventually had led her to a little room above the stables with a small square window showing moonlight on the cobblestones. He hadn't put on the light and he had difficulty opening the window. The room smelled musty at first but it was late May and the window soon let in the scents of lilac and hawthorn and she hadn't seen him for a while. Nor, as a matter of fact, did she want to see him ever again.

Even during the bumpy drive back to town in the back seat of a little Fiat designed for midgets, she knew she was pregnant. Maybe you always knew. Her mother had said she always knew and she'd been pregnant eight times. It was, her mother said, God's will. But God's will permitted contraceptives to be invented also and now it seemed rational to make the bearing of a child (whether in marriage or outside it) one's own will also. Once more she examined her body, imagining the gross changes of late pregnancy, the darkened milky nipples, the misshapen belly; worst of all the sinister pencil-blue stretch marks which (if one lived to be a hundred, her mother said) would never go away. Compulsively she took another shower, revelling in the warm mist of water in whose orbit she was happy again, as she supposed the embryo was happy in its watery element. Dry and dressed again, she went once more to count the pay cheques with which freedom would be bought.

A Friend of Don Juan

The straps cut sharply into his collarbones and a part of the steel frame lay unkindly against his vertebrae. Heavy mist which had blown in over Bray Head beaded his eyebrows and when he bent to the slope, water stung his eyes. Far ahead, on the long straight before you got onto the shoulder of the mountain, Dermot and Rachel played careless as children, in a gap of sunshine from which the mist had peeled away. William stopped for a moment to watch them, and they waved to him before striding on arm in arm, jerseys removed and knotted around their waists. He might as well be a porter for all the attention they paid to him, but then he should be used to that. In all the years since he and Dermot had come down from college together, the girls were changing constantly, but never the situation.

Bracing himself, he took the remaining hilly tussocks between him and the straight bed of a little stream, ignoring the pressure of the rucksack and his stinging watery eyes. If that skinny Rachel could carry it from home to the bus-stop, he could get it to the top of this mountain without too much bother. Coming down, it would certainly be lighter. It might even be carried by

Dermot, who frequently offered help when the need for it had practically vanished. This however was unlikely. He would be fooling around with Rachel on the way down, in playful mood probably, with her hair perhaps opened out of its long plait and wrapped around his own neck, and he would be singing at the top of his voice.

Dermot might play at independence but he could never get far without him in most circumstances. The man would frequently come out penniless, with only a cheque book as a proof to the world that he was not really without money. William never saw him short. Even when he made promises to two women for the same evening, William could be relied on to sort out the situation. Just as, at the end of every affair, William could be relied on for help towards a smooth exit.

Sometimes he couldn't remember clearly the faces of the girls who had wept out their loss of Dermot into his tweed jacket, but he could remember their names. Even in college there had been Mary and Sarah and Fidelma and Hilary and Joan; and Eithne, of course, the wife of a very junior lecturer. By way of breathing space after that brief but extremely scandalous affair (for which in justice Dermot could not be held wholly responsible), William had advanced the air fare to Germany, where money for a Greek holiday could be earned by factory work. In Greece he had offered Dermot the benefit of his somewhat unoriginal but useful advice. From the time of Helen of Troy onwards, no good had come to any man from helping himself to a slice of cut cake. All right, so wives had had their problems and they were sometimes available and seldom disappointing. But they were always more trouble than they were worth, and breaking with them was twenty times more emotionally charged than breaking with a girl. To everything Dermot said yes, of course William was right, and until the advent of the American girl, Mary Louise in Crete, he had been the best and most rational of companions. During the Mary Louise episode he had been considerably less trouble than in similar circumstances at home, and when he passed on to an English art student named Jennifer from Croyden, Mary Louise had been unusually generous to William.

In fact his ears still burned whenever he remembered that she had said his face was straight out of Rembrandt, not beautiful exactly but warm and reassuring. She said she liked prominent teeth that no American dentist had ever been allowed to reduce to the conformity of everybody else's, and no, a large nose the shape of his did not worry her too much. All this by way of a prelude to proving it couldn't possibly have worried her at all. William smiled at the astonishing memory, and set off briskly in the direction of his friends.

Rachel was sitting on Dermot's rolled-up jersey and he had one of her boots off, her bare foot resting between his knees. William smiled, remembering she had held out longer than anybody else against him – fully three months now.

"What's wrong?"

"Nothing that a plaster won't fix," Dermot said, business-like. "You've got one, haven't you?"

Of course he had. He bent to examine the blister, which had already broken, and then he made his selection from several plasters in his pocket. Rachel winced when he touched her foot. Stray wisps of blonde hair had escaped her thick plait and curled childishly around her face, beads of mist clinging to them.

"I won't hurt you," William assured her, "hold on." Dermot held the foot in the right position until the sticking plaster with its soothing lint was in place. Rachel sighed.

"Sweet William," she said, smiling at him. She had babyish teeth and a downy freckled face. Her bones were light as a bird's and he hardly noticed her weight when she allowed him to pull her up by one hand. Dermot, his eyes straining towards the sea, hushed them suddenly.

"Listen," he said.

They listened in the warm damp air but heard nothing except the wind in the heather that sounded like the distant wash of the tide. Suddenly Dermot mimicked a cuckoo's call, liquid and accurate, and again he motioned them to silence. Then they heard it coming from the woods outside the village.

"Cuck-coo. "

"Summer is coming in," Rachel sighed happily. "First time I've heard the cuckoo for three years. He belongs to school holidays."

"Neither of you heard him the first time?" Dermot asked a little contemptuously. Neither of them had, and he looked smug before hooking his arm through Rachel's and attempting to walk her off.

"Wait," Rachel said, "I've got apples." The mist was by now unmistakably thinning around them, and yellow spills of sun dazzled back at them from the distant sea. They sat down on a rock.

Rachel took off her blue cotton shirt and, still

munching, lifted up her closed eyes to the sun. Underneath she was wearing a tee-shirt of the same blue, cut away from thin freckled shoulders. Dermot removed his shirt too, and William felt his own cling to the prickly skin under the rucksack, under the tweed jacket. Even if he were not the official carrier he wouldn't shed his clothes anyway, however hot the day might become, because he had never learned to do things like that naturally.

He smiled however as he pulled back again into the slope. Without Dermot he wouldn't even have heard that bird, or earned that Sweet William from Rachel. Once he had tried climbing Djouce alone and for a while had savoured his freedom from tackle. In his pocket were only some fruit, some chocolate, and a change of socks. His mother had warned him he had to be careful with feet like his, if he ever aimed to court a girl. It had been a warm July day, with tender hazy sunlight and a small breeze. He hadn't enjoyed it.

But today the countryside opened and bloomed about him. The bitter almond smell of the gorse stung his nostrils. Was it Dean Swift who had said it smelled like the marriage bed? A skylark spun crazily above his head, the spiral of its song winding back down to him. He remembered Djouce again, when the day had been more beautiful, but it hadn't been the same. He had been free and it had been flavourless, nothing to involve his attention or to spur him into disapproval. He didn't really approve of Dermot's activities and especially of the present game with Rachel, whose parents had no doubt taken care for all of her nineteen years that she would meet none but nice Jewish boys with honourable intentions.

Until she went to college, that is. Until in her second year as a law student a celebrated former chairman of her debating society – Dermot – had been invited back to take over a rather important public discussion. William had attended, and he had seen the opening gambit of the familiar game. Absolute attention to every word that Rachel said. An adroit piece of public gallantry which Rachel had not rejected. The careful invitation to supper afterwards with both of them. How could the girl have known? William had even detected her slight surprise at his presence, but that was familiar ritual too, if only she had known it.

There were times when William felt he must know how God felt, having seen everything before. It was possible to intervene, but the rules forbade it. You watched. You assisted if asked. You waited. You offered consolation or understanding at the end, and these were your functions. You didn't overstep them. Once William's own elderly father had said to him in bafflement, "What sort of fellow fritters his life away playing gooseberry for a pup that will find himself a lonely old man at the end of all his andrew-martins? Let you go out and find yourself a nice girl before it's too late and marry her while that fellow is still gaping at you. Then your poor mother can rest easy."

Rest easy? Did she fear he was gay by any chance?

William smiled at this bizarre idea and also at the ingenuousness of the old man, maker of a safe middle-aged marriage himself. As if there were no more to it than that. As if it were so easy to be satisfied, to satisfy. He glanced up to where the others should be, but once again they had vanished into the mist that was perpetually forming and breaking above a certain height. At his level it was still warm and sunny but, looking back, he saw the sister mountain suspiciously close, as if it had taken several strides across the valley. It all meant rain, sooner or later. Maybe so late that they would be safely down and even on their way home by bus. Dermot and Rachel, unencumbered, might even be on top by now.

They were not, however. Breasting the next slope, William saw them waving to him. They were taking a rest, leaning up on their elbows in the heather. "Look over there for a change," William panted when he reached them at last, "and tell me what you see."

"The little mountain I climbed with the Hebrew group last year," Rachel said, pleased.

"I see rain," Dermot said, "but I don't see it soon. I may not even see it until we're all safe at home."

"That's what I think too," William agreed. "We could, of course, be wrong." He eased off the murderous rucksack and Rachel offered him her sympathy and, reaching into another pocket of the rucksack, some chocolate. They munched and complimented her on her foresight. Rachel blushed.

"My mother packed, actually – all of it," she said. "Just because I have five brothers and no sister, she thinks she has to keep on making up to me for something or other. I tell her if I had a sister we'd probably fight like cats, just like all the other sisters I knew in school, but she won't believe it. Says she never fought with her sisters."

"I never had anybody to fight with," William said, "I'm a child of aged parents."

"Accounts for his slightly neurotic attitude to normal things," Dermot said smoothly, "but he does the best he can. We mustn't blame him."

"So how many in your family, Dermot?" Rachel smiled. "You told me once but I've forgotten."

"Two brothers and a sister – all married, poor sods. Time we were moving on, friends. No place for dawdlers, this mountain."

"I'll carry my own rucksack for a while," Rachel, a little subdued, said to William, "it's ridiculous letting you carry everything. "

"I'm used to the weight of it now," William said, "in fact I don't even feel it heavy. But thanks all the same."

"Like me to take it for a bit?" Dermot offered spuriously and was ignored.

This time William set the pace, proudly aware of the weight he was carrying, even pleased about it. He didn't look back or pause until, almost an hour later, he had reached the last stretch of loose boulders. By then he was right inside the cloud which billowed moistly around him. Looking back, he saw them a quarter of a mile away, Dermot fastening a scarf about Rachel's head, both of them wearing jerseys again.

From that point on the rain grew steadily heavier and the landscape was blotted out. He stooped to pick up a stone for the cairn, hoping Rachel was being duly warned about the danger of twisting her ankle, and that Dermot would not climb gallantly ahead of her to show her the way and send a couple of hundredweight of loose granite crashing into her knees. But he decided not to look back. Eyes closed against the stinging rain, he clambered blindly up. Simply, it was a job that had to be done. He knew this climb so well anyhow that he didn't need his eyes. When he reached the end of the boulders, half an hour later, the cairn was in sight, and then he did look back. Rachel was still on her feet at any rate, and Dermot had a hand on her spine, steering her up. Their heads were bent into the rain.

By the time they came shouting and dripping up the last few paces, he had a fire going, against all reason, and the shouts turned into cheers. They finally squatted around the fire together and Rachel unpacked the food. Into their frozen fingers she put rolls of fresh bread with a filling of savoury herring, and these were followed by pastry with chicken and mushrooms. William thought of the unknown woman whose guests, in a sense, they were. Rachel poured dry white wine into waxed paper cups, and by the time she had topped the picnic with Passover biscuits, there was Bewley's coffee for them in the billycan. It was hot, black and comforting, and Rachel was able to produce little lumps of sugar in paper packets – "I collect these whenever I go on a plane," she explained.

"You have absolutely no idea what it's like to look down on a waterfall," Dermot assured Rachel. "It should be over there. We'll come back again on a good day and I'll show you. It can't be described."

On the way down, Dermot told Rachel to go ahead while they found a tree. She nodded, and started off alone. Presently Dermot took William's arm and winked. "It will be too late for the last bus when we get down," he murmured. "Remember to back me. Our lone stand against the Age of the Automobile has its advantages, no?"

161

"I'm having no part in this," William heard himself saying in some surprise, "Jacob worked seven years if you remember for the other Rachel. Then seven more when her old man substituted the ugly sister. You've only known this Rachel for three months."

"Longer than I've known anybody else under similar frustrating conditions," Dermot leered amiably.

"Look," William pleaded, "she's Jewish, and an only daughter. Her decent mother packed all that lovely food for us. One of their prophets recommended the burning of girls who make love before marriage."

"The Jews have civilised themselves quite considerably since then," Dermot smiled. "Besides, they don't burn such girls now, there are too many of them. It would be wasteful, don't you think?"

"Leave her alone," William urged. "You've behaved like a fucking bastard often enough and will do again. Leave this one alone – she's not much more than a baby. Jewish girls live a more sheltered life than ours do, remember."

"Poor Jewish girls! Are you kidding?" Dermot laughed loudly, "Are you under the impression that nobody has ever made a serious pass at Rachel?"

"I'm suggesting nothing of the kind – after three months with you. But remember I know your cat and mouse games pretty well – she doesn't. If she did she probably wouldn't be here at all."

"Nevertheless you must credit her with the ability to decide her own fate for herself," Dermot said lightly, and launched himself on the downward track.

At the little pub, bright and warm in the surrounding darkness, they drank hot whiskey and lemon and Rachel

162

seemed drowsy. Dermot ordered another round which Rachel sipped more slowly, un-plaiting her hair between sips.

"How's the sore heel?" William asked her.

"I don't even notice it, thanks to you. You made a great job of it. " Drowsily she smiled at him and he said, "It was nothing."

"On the contrary, it's what we bring him for, things like that," Dermot grinned.

"When will we be home, William?" It was perhaps a slight reproof to Dermot that the question was not addressed to him, but it was Dermot who answered anyway.

"No home for us tonight, love. Last bus has already gone, thanks to how slow we were in the rain. Not to worry, because they'll be able to put us up here snugly enough. And William has his American Express card, haven't you, William? How's the hair drying out?" He lifted up great golden handfuls into the firelight and let them go again. William's face was tickled by the downward fall and his nostrils teased by the steamy scented bathroom smell.

"Almost dry," Rachel sighed. "It's so warm in here." When Dermot put out an arm to her she settled back drowsily on to his shoulder but still smiled with the babyish teeth at William.

"Won't they be worrying about you at home?" William said stubbornly, ignoring Dermot's furious face above the girl's head. "They are expecting you home, aren't they?"

"Of course," Rachel said, shaking herself suddenly awake like a child. She stood up. "I must phone them. Excuse me."

"Wait," William heard himself saying, "It's not absolutely necessary to phone. Dermot's forgotten about the late bus that passes here from Wexford. It will have us in about half ten."

"Listen to him, Rachel. That's the summer timetable he's thinking of, and it doesn't begin until next month."

"It began two weeks ago at Easter," William said levelly. "So take your choice, Rachel."

"Meanwhile I'll ask the curate if he can put us up," Dermot said smoothly. "Let William go if he pleases for the bus that I know won't come." Whistling, he rang the bell and the curate sidled in, then shook his head doubtfully at Dermot's question.

"I'll have to ask your woman inside," he said, vanishing.

"You can ask the curate when he comes back about the bus, too," William said quietly. "Before Rachel phones, perhaps?"

"I think I'd better phone now – just in case," Rachel said. It was obvious to Dermot that she had become uneasy. Dragging her climbing boots a little, muscles already stiffening even in the warmth, she loped over to the door and smiled a peculiar pacifying smile at both of them before going out.

"You have a fucking nerve," Dermot grated. "Playing God was never part of your act, remember?"

"Acts can change," William said. "Sometimes the second half is even better than the first. I'll take Rachel back on the bus myself if that's how she wants it."

"I have an odd feeling that's not how Rachel wants it," Dermot grinned, draining his whiskey. "Nothing more

164

disappointing for God than when salvation is refunded, William, old pal."

"We'll see," said William.

Both their eyes were on the door. The curate sloped in first to say the boss had said it was OK if the two men would share a room, and then they waited, glaring at one another, for the scrape of Rachel's boots on the tiles outside.

France Is So Phoney

It's only that first lunchtime I remember clearly. There were a few others while the wind lasted and it was better to eat indoors. They all I think ended much the same, though the details are forgotten. But that first day the sun went in almost comically on cue when we were coming up the steep track from the beach and then you realised the wind was quite cold as well as unpleasant: the mistral, that blows like a threat over the summer people for a few days and then is gone.

Unlike the French who like to keep their rooms dark, we had opened all the shutters that morning and so the apartment was full of the lost sun's heat, welcoming. It had a faint delicious smell of Gauloises and coffee and maybe the last onion soup some Frenchwoman had cooked in the kitchen. It had white walls and white carpets; the furniture was dark and Spanish-looking and there were contemporary paintings everywhere. One of them I remember was by Arthur Armstrong, redolent of rain and home. Coady who had lent us the place went to all the more exclusive previews and bought what he fancied at the right price before the herd got in.

Denis unwrapped his long stick of bread ("It's called a 'grande', Emily, in case you are ever wondering what to ask for in the shops,") and fetched a bottle of Listel from the fridge. When I came back from my shower he was engrossed again in Midi Libre with the wine at his elbow and a piece nibbled off the bread in front of him. He didn't look up when I fetched cheese from the fridge, plates, glasses and a bowl of apricots. The window was a curved bay overlooking the sea which now looked choppy as along the west coast at home although it was still a patchwork of blues. Over the third glass of wine we began to talk inevitably of Sarah, to wonder if she might be lunching off identical fare in Paris, to wonder whether she was alone by choice or with the friends she could command anywhere. Companionably we talked on to the end of the wine, and then he asked for coffee.

"Later," I said, not able to keep from smiling. I had slipped without knowing it into a sensual mood which belonged in essence to long ago when Sarah was small, before I had learned to be cautious and not to court rejection. He looked up alarmed from his newspaper. "We are not in any hurry, are we?" I said.

Later ... we are not in any hurry. The phrases themselves belonged to a sexual life he had clearly forgotten although I had not. At times I felt all I had to do was stage-manage everything a little better and we might be back there again. We were perhaps back there again. But his hand reached for the cigarettes and mine for the matches, because once again this was all I could do for him.

"Aren't you tired after your long swim? Would you not like me to concoct some of my special coffee brew?"

I shook my head, desperately sorry I had begun this. His brown face in the matchlight was worried, his eyes predictably evasive. He suggested if I wasn't tired we might go and look at the museum which had a quite famous Roman section. It obviously was no afternoon for the beach. Besides, even if it had been, more sun would be bad for us, he said.

We went to the museum. It was an eighteenth century town mansion of beautiful proportions whose upper salons were furnished exactly as they would have been originally, complete with Aubusson carpets and old silken curtains. A thick journal bound with tooled leather was open on a davenport, sharpened quill ready beside it. You fancied that the nobleman who had travelled home in the silk-lined sedan chair we had seen in the hall might at any moment come in to record the doings of his day. His lady's harp glittered like gold in a corner of the room and it would have been easy to spend a whole day just browsing among the furniture and the dozen or more Vernets which lined one wall.

Denis however was bored by detail and irritated by the elderly voluble American couple who shared the place with us. He said all this could be found anywhere in France, for heaven's sake, a lot of it could be found in the Vendrons' chateau. What was special about this museum was the Roman section. So we hunted for that through passages with worn floors of honey-coloured stone, hollowed outside every door by feet that had hesitated before going in. Denis was annoyed to discover at last a plan of the house which we had overlooked because of the sedan chair in the hall. The Roman section was in the basement. I left him studying the plan and wandered down there myself. The stairs below hall level were of wood, shallow, worn, and lovely to descend. But the basement floors themselves were monastic looking, of rough stone tiles. There was nobody except a tall plump American in blue denims studying the Roman remains. He ambled across to me almost at once, his white tombstones flashing in the fleshy face. He was wearing open sandals, and his toe nails were long and dirty.

"Show ya something," he said good-humouredly as though I had known him all my life, "ancient gods had their problems too." One finger between my shoulder-blades, he guided me to a small creamy marble Apollo about two feet high. The face under its scultpured curls was perfect and rather beautiful but time or some other vandal had removed a nipple, one finger from the outstretched hand, and all of the genitals except a single testicle.

"Whaddya know," the soft mid-Western voice was saying. "Leave a guy to face the world wearing one nut, no more."

This was where Denis entered the conversation. His rope-soled shoes had made no noise coming in. "For all you would be able to understand, he might prefer to have his brainpower unimpaired. Look at the head. No brain damage, you see."

The American, to give him his due, summed up the situation in one flash of the handsome eyes from my left hand to Denis's face. Murmuring agreement, he was suddenly not there any more. Denis and I collapsed in laughter. I remember the rest of that afternoon as mainly harmonious. Despite a high-rise housing development outside the town, the centre was intact and mostly medieval, narrow cobbled lanes with washing strung across them, balconies full of babies and gossiping women. The main streets however were eighteenth century like the museum, broad and beautiful with fountains playing among the shrubs of the traffic islands. It was a town which had grown up around its ancient university, some of whose schools were older than those of the Sorbonne. It had a theatre and a concert hall and a large population of apparently contented fully integrated coloured students. In the main square cafe where we stopped they chattered in voluble French all around us – Algerians, perhaps?

"I never thought I'd come to France again after Algeria," Denis said, frowning.

"On that reckoning one could never go to Portugal or Greece or Britain or Germany – most of the world in fact would be out." He nodded, unwilling for argument, and played with the water they always served here with coffee. Under the striped awning the persistent cool wind crept. It wasn't really a day for sitting around.

"You don't know where the post office is," he said suddenly. "You should know."

"Have they stopped delivering mail in France?"

"It's a nice walk anyhow – I'll show you," he pleaded. "There's an alley full of cats on the way."

We went walking again.

The alley full of cats had pots of geraniums too, standing in the stone doorways, and again, overhead, the washing hung out to dry, clothes much newer and cleaner-looking than those of poor families at home.

Denis tried to stroke his favourite kind of marmalade cat but the creature retreated in terror into a hallway which was full of children's voices. The next cat did the same but at last he cornered a grubby white kitten with one black ear and sore eyes.

"They aren't used to being fussed over," I reminded him. "Remember Françoise when she first came to us, how bored she was by the attention we paid to our cat?' We were off again on familiar ground, remembering. Denis stroked the kitten with gentle persistent hands until it began at last to purr. He wondered how lonely our Simpkin was. I wondered if Sarah's friend was remembering to come in and feed him every day as she had promised. We wondered if perhaps we should have sent the animal to stay with the local vet while we were away.

"Remember the year he escaped and ran home to an empty house when we were in Kerry?"

"Not ran," Denis corrected, "he made his way very slowly indeed. Remember we reckoned it took him ten days?"

"Yes, I remember. He always was a fool."

Remember, remember. That was the year Denis had taken on Coady, fresh from college, and allowed him slowly to take over the office, handle all the major commissions himself, phase out the rest of the partners until (apart from the name) it was Coady's business, Coady's show. Ryan and Coady. More and more they were designing office blocks now, each, in my opinion, more hideous than the last. Georgian houses were falling one by one to the bulldozer, shadily acquired by the clients who got planning permission to rebuild even more shadily still. They applied again and again with donations to party funds timed to coincide with the latest appeal and eventually (however long it took) planning permission was granted even in areas scheduled for preservation. Ryan and Coady did what was regarded as a good stylish job, never cutting costs on popular touches like commissioned sculpture in the entrances or *cotoneaster horizontalis* in the patios behind. The clients invariably arranged for official openings at ministerial level which were noticed (with photographs) in the daily newspapers. More and more these days Denis was taking a back seat, refusing to make decisions, often electing to do site work which the most junior surveyor could have attended to without difficulty – the sort of work in fact which Sarah was doing now in her third year. All this could not be talked about so we discussed Simpkin instead.

Denis sat down on the steps with the kitten cradled in his lap. "Have you a tissue in your bag?" he asked me, and when I gave him one he tried to clean the cat's eyes, laughing when it suddenly lashed out at him before vanishing into the gloom. I offered him another tissue to deal with the blood but he shook his head and licked it away. The cathedral clock struck five.

At the post office the official summed Denis up impatiently as the man who had bothered her earlier.

"Rien du tout, monsieur."

"Allez voir encore, s'il vous plaît, madame."

"Rien," said the woman implacably.

Outside it was quite suddenly warmer and windless. Before we reached the fine Romanesque bridge its stone was golden in the late sun and in its shadow the eternal game of "boules" was in progress. Elderly men in straw hats – worn always I was to learn in sun or cloud – poised and estimated and threw and argued over almost every shot. If you closed your eyes the hard pock of one metal ball against another, surprisingly like the sound of croquet, brought you back to the novels of Trollope and Thackeray. But that was in another country. Only the sound was the same.

I linked my arm through Denis's and led him under the bridge to the public park whose entrance was a miniature Arc de Triomphe. It was so warm I threw off my jacket and tried to part Denis from his but he hated to shed clothes. What you missed here was birdsong, he remarked, and he was right, of course. No birds sang. Instead there was the plash of fountains and children's voices in the labyrinth of little paths through the shrubberies, and everywhere of course the croaking of frogs. We climbed a stone plinth and walked between the legs of an equestrian bronze of Louis XIV, and then we looked down at the flower-pot roofs of the town, then at the spires of the cathedral we hadn't yet visited. Beyond it, far beyond, were hazy mountains and below us, to the left, the half-moon of the sea.

I should buy food, I thought idly, and as though he had heard, Denis said we'd eat out tonight. It would be a pleasant evening for strolling. Also there would be music in the park tonight – had I noticed the poster? I hadn't, of course. It was he who hardly looked yet noticed everything except my occasional moods of despair. I was astonished he should suggest eating out, he who hated any ceremony

173

outside his own four walls. Now he seemed actually to be enjoying the prospect of dinner in town.

Long before the end of the meal I felt happy and hopeful. One always forgets how disappointing all holidays are in the beginning before some sort of ritual is established. From today it would be all right. I knew it as Denis ordered another bottle of rosé and indicated the label. "Bouzique," I read.

"It's situated on the salt lagoon of Sète," he said. "I'm going to take you there one day." It sounded proprietary, like long ago. I'm going to take you there one day. As a student he had hitched over most of Europe whereas I had not. He wanted to show me everything he had seen, all the subjects of his bulging sketch books. We had not, in fact, travelled very much after Sarah was born.

"The village of Bouzique," he went on, "is chiefly known for the unusual way they have of catching shellfish. When we go you can watch it." It was I who collected guide books, he who kept in his head every stray scrap of local information he had ever come across. "You might even like to eat the wretched molluscs they catch."

"Why not you too?"

"Food I endure," he said, "holiday food in particular. But I admit endurance becomes a positive pleasure where this wine is concerned."

"Maybe we could take some home with us."

"I don't think it would travel. Too light. The colour is curious. Colour of an onion skin."

Here was the precision that had made him so good as a student. With a minimum of equipment he could have produced a working approximation to that exact shade in his sketches long ago. His mother once showed me a folio of them jealously preserved. The year he won the McKenzie Fellowship. His final year's win of an open competition for a concert hall in Dublin. The model for that was gathering dust in her dead drawing room. The plans for it were filed away for all eternity in the municipal offices of Dublin's City Hall. I asked him a question I wouldn't have dared to ask if we hadn't been half way through the second bottle of wine. He gave me one of his rare smiles of pure enjoyment.

"You've forgotten. I showed it to you once and you liked it. Think."

What design that was ever really important to him had resulted in an actual building? Plans by the dozen I remembered. All of them had been altered or abandoned to his frequent despair. That was when he still cared.

"Doesn't the name Knocklacken mean anything to you?"

"That's the place you bypass on the road to Galway, isn't it? With terraced council houses all washed in different colours like the Kilkee seafront and a little main square with chestnut trees and a duck pond where the children play. Pines climbing up behind the houses. It isn't really like a council estate at all because ... I'm sorry. Oh God, I'm sorry Denis."

He was broadly smiling now as he continued. "It isn't really like a council housing estate because I didn't think of it that way. I thought of it as somewhere people would like to live. For God's sake, I fought even over those chestnut trees. They had to be chestnuts because of conkers in the autumn, you see."

175

"I don't understand how I could have forgotten."

"Don't worry, love, nobody else remembers either." He spoke easily, completely without rancour. "But since you asked me, it did give me pleasure to see it materialise exactly as I'd planned. It still does. There's a new generation of teenage parents growing up there who don't want to leave unless they can find somewhere like it. They can't because there isn't anywhere like it. It cost too much. It only happened at all because of the change of government at that time and an ambitious poor bastard of a minister who steamrolled Knocklacken through before anybody realised what he was doing. He's out of office now although his government is in again. An alcoholic, naturally. I see him sometimes in Neary's."

Denis was laughing between sips of wine, as he often did when something distressed him. It was suddenly easy to talk to him, and I remembered with surprise all the times we could hardly exchange a word of any importance to either of us. He would talk to me about staff or cars; I would tell him neighbourhood gossip and there would be long silences before one of us mentioned Sarah. Then I would tell him her news – her friends' success at their exams or failure, affairs beginning or breaking up, the occasional shipwreck.

But that night when the waiter brought coffee I felt I could have asked him anything, such as why he never wanted sex anymore or why he didn't shoulder off Coady. Pay him off if necessary. I started with the second subject and his face creased slightly. Then he laughed, drank off the whole tiny cupful and ordered more.

176

"Je voudrais une tasse, s'il vous plait," he said to the waiter with appropriate gestures, "pas demi-tasse."

"D'accord, monsieur. Et madame?"

"Ça va, merci."

"All of a sudden," said Denis, smiling across the table, "you look like Mary Kate."

Where in God's name was the sequence? I tried to stop my face from freezing and succeeded tolerably well, I think. I still had half a glass of wine left so I drank that slowly to buy time. But the question I wanted to suppress came out all the same.

"She is the reason why you keep fussing about the post, isn't she?"

"Sarah might some time be in some sort of trouble too, remember, and be glad of help from somebody like me."

"She would phone you if she were. Why don't you answer me?"

"Mary Kate," he articulated slowly, "is a very frightened little girl who needs to be sorted out quite often. I'm a year or so older than her own father who isn't available. That's all there is in it, as you know perfectly well."

Now I was beyond stopping myself though I knew how he would hate what I had to say. "Even if her father were here she wouldn't want to go to bed with him. She obviously does with you."

"Don't be silly. I sort her out, as I told you. She's sad and unstable and she knows her thesis will be terrible which doesn't help. She's not clever like Sarah and she's never had a proper home. You were sorry for her yourself when you asked her to stay, remember?"

177

"I never asked her to come back from California to stay again and again. I was merely obliging Dan O'Brien because he wrote that letter of introduction for her. You've let her assume disproportionate importance if you don't want to sleep with her."

"Young girls, like flowers, are only at their best for a little while," he said lightly. "Everybody should enjoy being à l'ombre des jeunes filles en fleurs while the magic lasts. It's detached enjoyment, nothing to do with sex." He was smiling again but it was clear his mind was miles away.

"Proust was talking about young men, in fact, but I suppose that's neither here nor there. If you were boss in your own company you wouldn't need such enjoyment," I nagged on, hating myself now. "Lucky Coady makes all the decisions (mostly wrong ones) and you never try to stop him. You sign agreements like a baby and then come home to write another long letter to Mary Kate. The business is going to ruins."

"Let it," he said lightly, "I'm fond of ruins – I'm a sort of ruin myself."

There were times when he looked like one but not always, not now. I put my hand on his in apology and suggested we walk back. Although I didn't entirely believe him about the American girl I wanted to believe him. It all seemed at that moment more than possibly true. Even more so during the stroll back hand in hand through the dusky yet brilliant gardens. It was Vivaldi this time and whole families idled together under the trees. The water which cascaded from the chateaux d'eau was bright blue and gold from invisible lighting below. A little band of

Algerians played mouth organs and danced around one of the fountains.

Allons dans les bois ma mignonette,
Allons dans les bois du roi ...

Then another group we passed were singing a song by Moustaki: *"Non, je ne suis jamais seul avec ma solitude."*

"France is so phoney," Denis grinned, "it's as though a stroll through the Phoenix Park actually yielded up leprechauns and crocks of gold. But it takes me in every time."

"Me too. That's why I love it."

The sweet solitude of the coast was phoney too, the lap of silky blue water against a deserted beach, a few sunshades still in position like sleeping butterflies. Nobody came here after seven, not even children as they would do at any Irish seaside resort. Here the older ones were at supervised summer camp in the mountains and the little ones had been tidied away out of sight by the Spanish au pair girls after an early supper. They were all asleep by now, probably. We climbed up to the verandah of the apartment by the beach.

No seabirds, of course. No sound but the lapping of water and the distant drone of cars.

"I saw a Corot of this place once," Denis said, as we stood to look back. "Not a very well-known or a very good Corot. It was painted in July 1904 and this beach was as empty as Mulrany. Not a house, not a parasol in sight. Half the canvas was an evening sky just like that one. There was one beached boat and a man walking near by with a dog at his heels. That was all."

179

"Where is this Corot?"

"I may have seen it in Paris – can't really remember. You won't, I think, find it in any collection of prints." We began to talk without sequence about Paris when we first saw it together, twenty years ago, but Denis inevitably went back to his first solo hitching trip abroad, the year before he graduated. All his real memories of places were of being alone. Almost our only mutual memories for turning over were of Sarah, always of Sarah.

"Would you like a nightcap," he said unexpectedly when we were inside.

"I'd love one."

After he'd poured the drink he sat down on the white carpet with a gesture of youth I hadn't seen for a long time. The windows were open to the theatrical moonlight, and a few summers ago I would have suggested a swim before going to bed. Now I knew it would break whatever mood the evening and the alcohol had built up between us. I couldn't as yet speak for him but I knew I desired the relaxed yet very slightly wary body as much as ever. He was smiling and he hadn't put on the lamp which was a good sign. I thought I wouldn't botch it this time so I made no move towards him, just sipped the cognac slowly and smiled back at him. Legs crossed in the strong reflected light, he looked a little unearthly with the curly hair silver and everything below it black, brows, lashes, eyes, beard.

Like two cats we sat watching one another for a long time. No sound but the sea. Then he made some remark about Coady's taste in booze and fearful lest the whole mood would collapse again like so many others I went

180

and put my hand into his open shirt to feel the heartbeats. Instantly he recoiled like a snail whose horns have been touched, and then he leaned over to light the lamp while he continued his joke about Coady. I couldn't explain or control the sudden fountain of tears and he mopped at them patiently as though I were Sarah. I gained control quickly enough and found words I hoped would strike home.

"If I were not a little drunk I'd have known better than to try with lustful impetuosity for the third time in eighteen months. I'm so sorry."

"I'm sorry too, Emily. But you should have known already how the idea fills me with revulsion – with you, with anybody. I've no hope that you will ever be able to regard this as a misfortune for me rather than an ingenious insult to you."

"You prefer men then, like Proust?"

Even as I made the stupid taunt I knew how inappropriate it was. He laughed with genuine enjoyment.

"I almost wish I did."

"So do I, Denis. So do I."

I left him laughing in the bright lamplight and went down by the balcony and the steep steps to the beach. The air was warm and the wind hadn't returned. I had been walking furiously along the shoreline for twenty minutes before I realised I was walking not in the direction of a furled sunshade but of a man watching the sea. The red bead of his cigarette and the curling smoke about him gave him a touch of the bizarre. Not Corot but Robert Ballagh would have loved to paint him. Without any of the denim clothes in which I had seen him earlier that day in the museum I didn't recognise him at first (all fat men when naked look much the same) but then I remembered his soft mid-Western voice and then the handsome smokey eyes.

"I can recommend that water for a swim right now," he said slowly, stubbing out the cigarette. "I can recommend it because I've been in one time already. Come try it with me lady, unless your husband is following you like last time?"

For answer I wriggled quickly out of my two garments and ran with him into the water, thinking that after a second swim even his toe nails might be clean.

End of the Line

It's the raspberries I remember best about that summer. There never was such a crop and I knew that Mr Bentley had decided to build his entire entertaining around them for a while. He phoned me one day and (obliquely as ever) giggling slightly, intimated that he still had far too many raspberries and we would have to help him out with them again. Who else was coming? I could hear the caution in my own voice, even although I knew that Mr Bentley's parties of one sort or another were rarely intolerable. It was just that he had made himself responsible for quite a few dull people who were so obsessed with their own problems that they tended to drive other people away. Would I care to bring Jerry along as a peace gesture, Mr Bentley asked suddenly, and he giggled uneasily when I said I certainly would not. He said no more except that if Saturday would suit me it would be fine for him and not to bother eating before I arrived some time around midday.

Mr Bentley lived where he had always lived ever since I was at school and went to him for extra piano lessons. He lived in a large stone house of amazing ugliness except for the largely wild garden. You approached it through a leafy gap between numbers eighteen and twenty of a handsome road in Donnybrook. Almost immediately you found yourself confronting the remains of a beautiful ironwork gate with "Hazeldene" inscrolled on it. This could be confusing to a newcomer because it was not the entrance to a conventional driveway. Elegantly designed bungalows were scattered to right and left behind their screens of copper beech or poplar. Some of them dated from the nineteen-twenties and most of them were supposed to be guarded by the large somnolent dogs who lifted a lazy eye at strange footsteps and sometimes came over wagging their tails. Everywhere there was the silence of all those trees and you felt vaguely that if there had to be bungalows there they should have been Indian Empire style with maybe a dozing ayah rocking in the porch and the breathing jungle just a short distance away in the intense heat.

There was nothing colonial in that sense about Mr Bentley's home when you came upon it at last in its circular gravelled drive. It was large, Cromwellian-looking and fortressy, made of cut-stone that had seen better days. Lichens had invaded it and the dampness had made strange colours and patterns on the wall. A dead Virginia creeper still held on with its bleached white arms. Partly wild since the last live-in family gardener had been put away into a home and the last ffrench-Morris had died in Bournemouth it was, thanks to Mr Bentley, a paradise garden in other parts. There were rose beds that I could smell as soon as I stepped onto the drive and there were little brilliant shrubberies scooped out of the brambles and bamboos, which blazed with jonquils and crocuses in early spring. In summer there were big flowering things like hydrangeas which took care of themselves and there was every imaginable kind of heather.

Each time Mr Bentley made another border or shrubbery he had to ask formal permission through the solicitors of the present owner, a building contractor who maintained distant but good terms with the few remaining tenants. Nobody had ever had to fend off a bribe to quit, but it was noticeable that there were no new lettings either. Mr Bentley had been given (on a mere request) permission to use some of the empty rooms for entertaining in whenever he wished, and I can remember a few good Christmas parties in gaunt candlelit rooms which he had transformed as though they were stage sets with trailing ivy and red ribbons.

His own flat was small and dusty and largely taken over by his grand piano and his bookshelves. He had never lived anywhere else since his mother died and left their joint home to a more favoured son in Canada. It was to this small flat I used to come as a schoolgirl, drawn in the right direction that first time by the hesitant tinkle of scales coming through the trees. Mr Bentley was firm as well as patient. Many of his students eventually won prizes and some of them were concert performers now.

I found him beaming among the raspberry canes from which a gentle steam was rising after last night's rain.

"They love it," he assured me. "Heat and moisture combined. They keep coming and ripening for me – pick a bowlful for breakfast and you have more berries on those same bushes for dinner. Welcome, Anna." His tufted white hair stood up straight on his head and his eyes were kind and blue as cornflowers. His wrecked teeth ought to have looked ugly but instead his smile was something people remembered. There was nothing in his face to suggest the disciplinarian that lurked behind it. "Find a bowl over there and come and help me, Anna."

I did as I was told although I would have preferred to sit on a fallen tree trunk and lift my face to the sun. I had always liked to close my eyes and listen to his garden. Bees among the roses and the fading cotoneaster blossoms. A grasshopper somewhere. The river rattling on over its pebbles at the end of the wall. The stretching and sighing of trees especially in the heat. But I knew this garden in every season. I liked it best in the depths of summer although I can hardly remember an idle moment there. I remember weeding, watering, dead-heading, picking roses for the house. I remember cutting shrubs back after flowering to strengthen them for next summer. All that.

"Who's coming?"

He gave me a name and I sighed.

"A very talented woman," he said firmly. "A very difficult life which she has triumphantly organised."

"That's her trouble," I sighed again. "Organisation. Who else?" He told me. It was going to be one of those days. "I can't stay very long," I said.

"But all the same I know you will, Anna. I need your help. Besides it's a special day."

"Every day is a special day to you," I grumbled and then gave myself up to the enjoyment of the raspberries themselves, so fragile in their ripeness, so moist and soft that they needed feather fingers to pick them. Piano fingers. I looked from my several ruined berries into Mr Bentley's bowl of beauties and then I looked down at his bony hands, no flesh anywhere except at the soft fingertips lightly coloured by the juices which he had not spilled. Mr Bentley would never be coarse the way my own father loved to be at times. "Handle those pears as tenderly as though they were virgins," he said to me once, to be instantly reproved by my mother. I went on picking berries in silent companionship for a long time, fingers tingling with the fine little thorny needles which protected the fruit.

"You made me forget what I was about to do when you arrived," Mr Bentley said, and before going into the house he took and emptied my half-full bowl into his own and gave it back to me. I went on picking, conscious now of the winey smell of the fruit as the sun strengthened to a burning point on the back of my neck. I had always felt secure in this garden, indeed in Mr Bentley's company. It was a place where I liked to come to forget the person I really was. When he came back he put an old straw hat on my head and another even more battered on his own. He had carried them one inside the other under one arm and an old portable gramophone (the sort you wind up) hung from the other. He had forgotten to bring back his bowl, so I went around to fetch that and even from indoors, in the chill gloom, I could hear the ravishing music, vaguely familiar and improved if anything by the tinny sound box of the old machine. I looked around at the tidy details of Mr Bentley's kitchen, his clean tea towels hanging up on the hooks, his big bowls of prepared salads, his plait of garlic hung from the casement window frame and his rows of spices. The music got louder and tinnier as I neared the raspberry canes and I found him standing with eyes closed and a sweet smile on his face.

"*Tod und Verklärung*, Anna," he said, shaking his head, and resuming his picking. "One of the divinest sounds of this century. Strauss wrote it when he was a stripling, you'll remember – what could he have known then of death and transfiguration? In fact he knew everything and the proof is (or I believe it is) that he reworked some of those themes into the *Last Songs* completed the year of his death. Sit down for a minute and listen. We have plenty of time to finish our picking before the others arrive."

So we sat down on a once-white garden seat and listened to the aching sweetness of the music that follows the troubled opening bars.

"Don't cry, Anna, but tell me about it, " Mr Bentley said. "Why don't you go back to your husband and see how it will be? You married him, after all. Things go wrong but the basic feeling must remain, I think. I don't, of course, know," he said modestly, patting my hand kindly.

"No you don't, Mr Bentley. We were married two years ago and already all that is over. He slurped his soup and grunted like a pig in bed and never came to the Concert Hall any more. And he only took one shower a week – every Saturday night – and he left his cigarette butts in the hand basin and he never disguised the fact that he hated my cat. Once he went home with a *man* after we'd gone out together to a party and he got somebody else to give me a lift home."

Silenced by this time, Mr Bentley looked dismayed at me for a moment before replying delicately.

"I hope he's careful about his health. That sort of life is very dangerous these times as we all know but you may be mistaken. Maybe if you had a baby," Mr Bentley said wistfully. "After a check-up for both of you, of course."

"No *thank* you," I shuddered with genuine horror. "You're a dear but you're so wrong it's pathetic. Let's get back to the raspberries."

"I'll talk to you later, Anna," Mr Bentley said gently. "Dry your eyes." He gave me one of his usual spotless handkerchiefs (did he do his own laundry too?) and we went back to our picking.

Delius appeared suddenly from the vegetable patch where he may have been lying asleep and licked my bare legs affectionately. He's an old once-white Scotch terrier who doesn't smell too good any more but he's part of Hazeldene and I've known him a long time. He ate a raspberry Mr Bentley offered him and he must be the only dog in the world who would do that. As we worked he waddled to the garden seat and lay down there in the shade of it, nose between his paws.

"It isn't as though I had any talent to fall back on," I said, coming to the middle row Mr Bentley and I were picking together, and suddenly looking into his face I knew if I'd had the choice of a father this is the man I would select to be mine. If he weren't basically so truthful he would have reassured me now but I wouldn't be interested in that sort of reassurance.

"You will always play to the great pleasure of those listening to you in a domestic setting," Mr Bentley said kindly. "That's not nothing, Anna. And if you can refrain from being so hard on yourself you will always play for your own considerable pleasure too. Will you not be satisfied as I had to be so long ago when I opted for teaching and that turned out to be a source of lifelong joy to me?"

He smiled his beautiful smile again under the old straw hat and it didn't matter that the teeth were gapped in his upper jaw while in his lower jaw they were worn down like those of an old horse. I shook my head and looked away and the old gramophone rattled into silence.

"Look, here's another treat for you," he said. "Listen to this. I think you haven't heard the Lucia Popp recording of the *Last Songs*."

The voice is beautiful beyond measure and so are the songs but I don't think anybody can ever have heard them to such advantage as I did that July afternoon in Mr Bentley's garden. They are voluptuous, languishing songs and the way she sings them makes you know it's all over.

But I wasn't going to cry again in view of the voices from the front of the house announcing the arrival of all those dull people whose problems would be placed before Mr Bentley whenever the chance arose. Sometimes you could see them watching for it. But I'll say this for them. They fell upon the meat ready for carving and they set about all the remaining work and they even carried out the kitchen table to place under the chestnut tree where everything was laid out temptingly in the shade. One of the women had brought a freshly baked salmon which she had done herself and another had whipped bowls of the cream they'd brought for the raspberries. A particularly tiresome man had brought a bottle of gin

– it was more usual to bring wine – because he said it improved the flavour of the raspberries. While we ate the wafers of beautifully carved beef (there was a master carver among the friends too) and the salmon and all the salads Mr Bentley had prepared, the raspberries lay bathing in a whole cupful of gin in a large blue bowl, their colour dimmed by a light dusting of castor sugar. I prefer raspberries with no sweetness but their own, but naturally the woman who had triumphantly organised her very difficult life had sugared them. Nevertheless, eaten with ice-cold Muscadet, they were very good.

Nobody who hasn't been given raspberries straight from the vines within an hour of picking knows what raspberries should taste like. Strawberries by comparison are mundane. It's true they come first but by the time summer is at height, they are already turnipy and flavourless. Raspberries are the true fruits of midsummer, and it was in Mr Bentley's garden that I first tasted them as they should be eaten. The taste of ripe raspberries at the moment when they melt between your teeth is what I remember best of that summer and I have reason to remember that summer. After lunch we lay around on the grass which earlier in the day had been cool and damp and was now parched by the sun. My shorts and tee shirt looked absurd among the elaborate summer dresses of the women but that was how I'd planned to look, among them but not of them. They all recoiled from Delius when he ambled around offering his welcome, and eventually the dog settled himself against my legs, his old fur smelly, scratchy and hot. But I could do that much for him if he liked to be there. He rewarded me by caressing my wrist

191

with a cold black nose, surprisingly moist and healthy. I could have lain in that garden forever, giving nothing except to the dog, listening to the bees in the lime trees to my left, to the rattling unseen river, to Mr Bentley's reasonable soft voice offering advice, even a solution or two.

I wished they would all go away, especially the gin man who wanted to know where my husband was. Eventually they did go, but not before the sun was low and thick and golden along the grass, not before they had carried everything back into the house including the table and put the kitchen to rights again. That's the kind of people they are. The gin man was the last to go after he had played Chopin softly and abominably on Mr Bentley's grand piano and invited me to accompany him to the theatre that night because he had a spare ticket. When I refused he went away civilly enough.

This had always been my time of day in the garden. We didn't talk very much. We rambled around picking up morsels of food or the odd paper napkin off the grass although truly the guests had tidied up pretty well.

We wandered over to a rose bed at exactly the hour when roses are at their best, breathing out the accumulated heat of the day, practically ready to talk to you. Almost all of Mr Bentley's roses were old-fashioned, chosen for their exact shape and colour but also for their perfumes. They shaded from creamy white at the edges of the circular bed through to pink and crimson and yellow and, at the centre, a few almost black roses. I liked the floppy pink tea roses best. Mr Bentley preferred what he called Crimson Glory, deeply red and velvety and smelling of heaven but with a tendency to hang its head in full bloom. You had to lift it up to look at it.

"Let's take a bunch of these up to Mrs Aylmer," Mr Bentley said suddenly, "and the rest of the raspberries. But wait, before we do, we must water the roses and then I want to show you something, Anna."

Watering roses after a long hot day is never a chore, they seem to stretch up and offer themselves for spraying and even the droopers sometimes lift their heads. Saying he would cut Mrs Aylmer's roses when they dried off a bit, Mr Bentley led the way past his vegetable garden and through a wilderness of brambles and thistles to a little clearing near the river wall. Here he indicated a few straggling green plants which seemed to me quite unremarkable. But Mr Bentley smiled triumphantly.

"Planted them last autumn and always forgot to show you. Hazels, Anna. In years to come in this soft wet soil here will be hazelnuts for the picking and nobody will ever know or enjoy them except for a few gallant explorers from your old school! Imagine a Hazeldene without hazels!" he chuckled. "And yet I believe this garden has been without hazel bushes since it was laid out some hundred and fifty years ago, the time the house was built. Of course it could have been called after a lady named Hazel."

"That was a brilliant idea to plant those," I said, smiling at him. He looked down quite shyly in acknowledgement and giggled. Then he went back to cut the roses and on into the house to feed Delius.

The house, which could be icy cold in winter, seemed to hold all the heat of the long summer's day as we climbed the neglected staircase to Mrs Aylmer's. On both landings we passed tall windows overlooking the river and the setting sun. Its light filtered strangely through the dusty panels of deep blue and gold glass, and it changed Mr Bentley's face quite suddenly into that of an old man. I shivered slightly. There would be a long warm twilight when the sun went down, he predicted. Maybe if I wasn't in any hurry I might like to play a Bach trio with him before we made supper? We could forget about the viola and he'd play the fiddle to my piano. We would leave the window wide open and Mrs Aylmer could listen too. Her room was just above his, these two floors up.

There was an amazing blood-red sunset flooding across Mrs Aylmer's landing but no answer when we knocked at her door. The brass plate was handsome and brightly polished and it said "Florence Aylmer Speech Therapist/Consultations By Appointment". Was it because we hadn't an appointment that there was no answer, I wondered flippantly, but Mr Bentley was very worried, quite pale, I noticed, in a moment. He called "Florence!" several times and then asked me to wait while he went down to fetch the spare key she had given him "in case of emergencies." This, it seemed, was an emergency. I walked over to the window and felt the warmth of the last light of the day washing over me. I was irritated with Florence Aylmer whom I had never met because she was intruding by her silence. I noticed Mr Bentley had taken away his red roses and his raspberries as though he didn't expect to be able to deliver them. He was not.

We found Mrs Aylmer who was large and very old fallen sideways in her bed, her face purplish and her hands cold, but she was not dead. The oriental beauty and order of the room seemed in strange contrast to the ungainly figure. Mr Bentley tried his best to rouse her but he failed and asked me to phone 999 for an ambulance while he stayed with her. I tried to feel pity for this unknown old woman, speech therapist and widow of an art collector, young once and maybe beautiful, maybe even happy, but all I could feel was irritation that a lovely day which had not ended was now apparently over.

The ambulance men with great speed and efficiency arrived and carried her downstairs on a stretcher, all wrapped up in blankets. I watched in the driveway as they settled Mrs Aylmer into the ambulance, slammed the doors, got Mr Bentley to sign a paper and drove away under the trees. When I looked again at Mr Bentley I saw that he was shaking although his face seemed as immobile as the old lady's. I wondered if perhaps they had been lovers long ago or even before Mrs Aylmer had become so crippled with arthritis, but the more I thought about it the less likely it seemed.

"I'll make you a cup of tea," I said, smiling at him because it seemed the only thing I could do for him but he said, "No, Anna, no. We'll have a drop of something stronger tonight."

In the dusky music room he lifted down a bottle of whiskey from his wall cabinet and then he took down two heavy crystal glasses. I'd never seen him drink anything but wine before and I myself connected whiskey with two things only, hot lemony punch for winter colds as a child and the swinish snoring of my husband after futile attempts at copulation several nights a week. But I suddenly discovered I too was cold, because that was how Mr Bentley was. He handed me my glass with a hand that was still shaking and we sipped the hot spirit together without speaking. After several swallows Mr Bentley's drink was almost gone and he poured a little more into the glasses before replacing his bottle in the cupboard.

"Poor Florence," he said. "Poor Florence. If only I'd come up earlier, as I'd intended to – "

"No," I said. "It wouldn't have made any difference, you know it wouldn't."

"Perhaps you're right." He sighed as he switched on a lamp that had a dusty deep yellow shade but also he smiled at me.

"You know, Anna, I think this is the actual end of the line for this old house."

"How do you mean?" My heart dropped like a stone, and I felt like a dreamer who has missed several steps on the stairway. He smiled again, sipped his whiskey as though nothing were the matter and then he took a letter out of his pocket.

"I told you this was a special day, Anna. It's special because this came by post this morning."

Before I read it I knew exactly what it would say. Donlon and Company, Building Contractors, had instructed the writer to thank Mr Bentley for his careful attention in every respect to their property, but they now felt it was time to offer both him and Mrs Aylmer alternative accommodation in one of their developed properties.

"A service flat!" I said, shocked even before I finished reading the letter. He would find that the owners would be more than generous in the matter of rent in view of his long tenancy of a ground-floor apartment at Hazeldene but of course if he preferred to make his own arrangements about alternative accommodation there would be a sum of money forthcoming to compensate for the disturbance. The solicitor strongly advised Mr Bentley to go along with the first suggestion which in his opinion would be financially advantageous. He would be pleased to discuss personally etc.

Something suddenly struck me as I folded up the letter. "Did Mrs Aylmer get one of those this morning?"

"Yes she did. She phoned me and I went up to her. She was shattered. She's been a tenant here for thirty years, ever since her husband died."

"Don't you think this may have had something to do with –"

"I'm sure of it."

"She's old, " I said, anxious to convince myself as well as him. "It might have happened anyway. You're *much* younger, and I know it's awful but you'll, you'll ..." There it was, I was crying again, and Mr Bentley, far more normal looking now after the drink, was looking as concerned as ever for me.

"I'll be perfectly all right wherever I go – of course I will. Once I have transported my piano and my books and all my junk, what does the place matter? Home can be remade anywhere, Anna."

I know it was disgraceful, utterly shameful, but I was crying for myself now.

"Your new hazel bushes!" I howled. "Your raspberries and your roses and your vegetable patch. It's not *fair!*"

"Do you know, Anna, if they have a tither of wit they'll leave the roses and the trees and some at least of the little wilderness beside the river and then they can sell more expensive houses. Bet you they'll call them town houses of character and quality in a secluded woodland setting within ten minutes of the city centre. What do you bet?" said Mr Bentley, looking almost mischievous now. "Come on, Anna, dry your eyes and what's more important dry your fingers, my dear, and sit down at the piano. Why shouldn't we have our little night music after all, and then we can make supper and take Delius for his walk at the same time as we leave you most of the way home."

"Home?" I said, again shamefully, "I have no home but this."

Mr Bentley didn't appear to hear me. He was tuning his fiddle, seemingly quite absorbed and happy. Forcing my memory now I still have no clear recollection of the music, whether I played badly or well. What I remember of that last day at Hazeldene are the warm raspberries and their exact texture as they burst between your teeth. *Tod und Verklärung* on the old scratchy gramophone and the sun burning the back of my neck until Mr Bentley's old hat gave me its healing shade.

Memory and Desire

The television people seemed to like him and that was a new feeling he found exciting. Outside his own work circle he was not liked, on the whole, although he had a couple of lifelong friends he no longer cared for very much. The sort of people he would have wished to be accepted by found him arrogant, unfriendly, and not plain enough to be encouraged as an oddity. His wealth made him attractive only to the types he most despised. He was physically gross and clumsy with none of the social graces except laughter. Sometimes his jokes were good and communicable. More often they were obscure and left him laughing alone as though he were the last remaining inhabitant of an island.

Sometimes, indeed, he wondered if he spoke the same language as most other people, so frequently were they baffled if not positively repelled. He liked people generally, especially physically beautiful people who seemed to him magical as old gods. Sometimes he just looked at such people, not listening or pretending to listen to what they said, and then he saw the familiar expression of dislike and exclusion passing across their faces and he knew he had blundered again. Now for several weeks he had been among a closely-knit group who actually seemed to find his company agreeable. When the invitation had come he had been doubtful. He knew nothing about television and seldom watched it. But because his father's small glass-making business had blossomed under his hand and become an important element in the export market, the television people thought a programme could be made out of his success story, a then-and-now sort of approach which seemed to him banal in the extreme. He had given his eventual consent because time so often hung on his hands now that expansion had progressed as far as was practicable and delegation had left him with little to do except see his more lucrative contacts in Europe and the United States a couple of times a year.

The only work he would actually have enjoyed doing these days was supervising the first efforts of young glass-blowers. Two of the present half-dozen were grandsons of his father's original men. At a time when traditional crafts were dying out everywhere or falling into strange (and probably passing) hands, this pleased him. He tried to show signs of his approval while keeping the necessary distance right from the boys' first day at work, but this was probably one of the few places left in Ireland where country boys were shy and backward still, and their embarrassment had been so obvious that nowadays he confined himself to reports on them from the foreman. It had been different in his father's time. The single cutter and the couple of blowers had become personal friends of his father and mother, living in the loft above the workshops (kept warm in winter by the kiln) and eating with the family in the manner of medieval apprentice craftsmen. During holidays from boarding school they had become his friends too, gradually and naturally passing on their skills to him, and so listening without resentment to the new ideas on design he had in due course brought back with him from art school and from working spells in Sweden. Gradually over the years of expansion after his father's death he had grown away from the men. Now since the new factory had been built in Cork he knew very few of them any more.

The odd thing about the television people was that right from the beginning they had been un-awed and called him Bernard, accepting that he had things to learn about their business and that he would stay with them in the same guest house, drink and live with them during the shooting of the film, almost as though they were his family and he an ordinary member of theirs. It had irritated and amused and baffled and pleased him in rapid progression and now he even found it hard to remember what his life had been like before he knew them or how his days had been filled in. Their youth too had shocked him in the beginning; they seemed like children at play with dangerous and expensive toys. The director in particular (who was also the producer and therefore responsible for the whole idea) had in addition to a good-humoured boy's face an almost fatherly air of concern for his odd and not always biddable family. What was more remarkable, he could discipline them. The assistant cameraman who had got drunk and couldn't be wakened on the third day of shooting had not done it again. When Eithne, the production assistant, had come down to breakfast one morning with a streaming cold and a raised

201

temperature, Martin had stuffed a handful of her notes into the pocket of his jeans and sent her back up to bed, weeping and protesting that she was perfectly all right and not even her mother would dare to treat her like that.

Martin was very good with uncooperative fishermen, and with the farmer on whose land the original workshop still hung over the sea. A nearby hilly field had recently been sown with oats, and the farmer began with the strongest objection to a jeep laden with gear coming anywhere near it. He had agreed to it during preliminary negotiations, but shooting had in fact been delayed (until more money became available) and that field, the farmer said, was in a delicate condition now. If they'd only come at the right time – Martin it was who finally talked him around with a guarantee against loss which would probably land him in trouble back in Dublin. But Martin (the Marvellous Boy was Bernard's private label for him) would worry about that one when he came to it and he advised Bernard to do the same about his fear of appearing ridiculous in some sequences. Not even half the stuff they were shooting would eventually be used, Martin said, and anyhow he'd give Bernard a preview at the earliest possible moment. Bernard stopped worrying again. Most of the time he had the intoxicating illusion of drifting with a strong tide in the company of excellent seamen and a captain who seemed to know his business.

The actual process of remembering was occasionally painful, of course. His only brother Tom had been swept away by a spring tide while fishing down on the rocks one day after school, and at first Bernard hadn't believed any reference to it would be possible when the script finally came to be written. Martin had come back to it casually again and again however, and finally one day of sharp March winds and flying patches of blue sky he had stood with Bernard on the headland near the roofless house.

"Let me show you what I have in mind," Martin said gently, the south Kerry accent soft as butter. "It will be very impressionistic, what I've in mind, a mere flash. A spin of sky and running tides, a moment.

"If you'd prefer, it won't need anything specific in the script. Just a reference to this friendly big brother mad about fishing, who knew about sea birds and seals and liked to be out by himself for hours on end. Maybe then, a single sentence about the nature of spring tides. The viewers generally won't know that spring tides have nothing to do with spring. You may say we're telling them about a successful glass industry, not about the sea, but the sea takes up a large part of your own early background and this piece is about you too. I'd write you a single sentence myself for your approval if you wouldn't mind – just to show you what I think would work – OK?"

"'These are pearls that were his eyes' – you could end like that, couldn't you?" Bernard heard himself sneering and almost at once regretted it. The director actually blushed and changed the subject. In a few seconds it was as if the moment had never happened, but it seemed to Bernard that a kind of bond had been perversely established.

Two days later a spring tide was running and he watched a few sequences being shot that might well be used for the passage he knew now he was going to write. He walked away from the crew when he found he could no longer watch the sort of sling from which the chief cameraman had been suspended above the cliffs to get some of the necessary angles. The whole thing could have been done better and more safely by helicopter but Martin had explained about the problems he had encountered after overrunning the budget for the last production. It wasn't of course that he wanted necessarily to make Bernard's backward look a cheaper affair; you often got a better end result (in his own experience) by using more ingenuity and less money: he thought he knew exactly how to do it. The somewhat unconvincing argument amused and didn't displease Bernard, who thought it more than likely that something less conventional might finally emerge. The last he saw of the crew was that crazy young man, clad as always when working in a cotton plaid shirt, suspending himself without the benefit of the cameraman's sling to try to see exactly what the lens saw.

A fit of nervousness that had in it something of the paternal and something else not paternal at all made him walk the seven miles around to the next headland. He hadn't thought like a father for five years. For half of that isolated time he hadn't brought home casual male encounters either because nothing stable had ever emerged from them and more often than not he was put off by the jungle whiff of the predator and managed to change direction just in time. Now he tried to resist looking back at the pair of boys busy with their games which they apparently regarded as serious. The head cameraman was even younger than Martin. He had a fair freckled face and red hair so long that it would surely have been safer to tie it back in a girl's ponytail before swinging him out in that perilous contraption. Bernard turned his face again into the stiff wind and looked back at the receding insect wriggling above the foaming tide, man and technology welded together in the blasting sunlight. The weird shape drew back his eyes again and again until a rock they called the Billygoat's Missus cut it off and he was alone for (it seemed) the first time in several weeks.

For the first time as in a camera's framed eye he saw his own room at home. Tidy as a well-kept grave, it was full of spring light from the garden. There were daffodils on his desk. Spangles of light from the rocky pool outside danced on the Yeats canvas that took up most of one wall and struck sparks from the two early balloons which he treasured. Five poplars in a haze of young green marked the end of his garden. Beyond it, the sharp-breasted great Sugarloaf and eventually the sea. The room had been tidy for five years now. No maddening litter of dropped magazines, no hairpins, no shoes kicked off and left where they fell: left for the woman next morning to carry to the appropriate place in the appropriate room because she was born to pick up the litter of other people's lives, paid for it as the only work she knew. One night in a fit of disgust he had kicked into the corner a black leather clog, left dead centre on the dark carpet awaiting the exact moment to catch his shin. Uncontrolled fits of violence he despised. Recovering quickly he had placed the shoes side by side outside the door as though this were an old-fashioned hotel with a dutiful boots in residence. She had come in laughing later on, both clogs held up incredulously in her hand, laughing and laughing, tossing them finally up in the air to fall where they might before she left the room.

As perhaps she had done last night and would do again tomorrow. Wherever she was.

A rising wind drove before it into the harbour a flock of black clouds that had appeared from nowhere, and when drops of rain the size of old pennies began to lash down he sought refuge in the hotel which had been small and unpretentious in its comfort when he was a child. His father's clients had often stayed here. He had sometimes been sent on messages to them with his brother. Now the place had several stars from an international guide book and was famous both for its sea food and the prices that foreign gourmets were willing to pay for it.

He sat in the little bar full of old coastal maps and looked out at the sea; alone for the first time in two weeks he was no less content than in the casual company of the television people. Their young faces and their voices were still inside his head. As though on cue, Martin suddenly came through into the bar, also alone. The wind had made any more shooting too dangerous for today he said, and the girls had gone off to wash their hair. He had his fishing gear in the boot, but he doubted if he'd do much good today.

"Have lunch with me, then, and eat some fish instead," Bernard invited, and was amused to see a flash of pure pleasure light up the director's face. Beer and a sandwich usually kept them going until they all sat down together at the end of the day.

"This place has got so much above itself even since the last time I was down here that I expect to be asked my business as soon as I set foot inside the door," Martin grinned.

"They wouldn't do that in late March," Bernard assured him. "Neither the swallows nor the tourists have arrived yet, so I fancy even people in your state of sartorial decay would be encouraged."

Martin took an imaginary clothes brush out of the jeans pocket (too tight to hold any thing larger than a toothbrush) and began to remove stray hairs from that well-worn garment which had seaweedy stains in several places and looked slightly damp. The boy walked with a sort of spring, like a healthy cat, and there was no trace yet of the flab which his pint-drinking would eventually bring. He ate the bouillabaisse and the fresh baked salmon which followed with the relish of a child brought out from boarding school for the day and determined to take full advantage of it. He praised the Alsace wine which was apparently new to him and Bernard decided that one of the great remaining pleasures of money was never to have to worry about the cost of any thing one suddenly wanted to do.

Bernard listened abstractedly to a little house politics over the coffee and then at the end of the first cognac he spoke one unwary line about buying all those bandy little boss men for a next birthday present for Martin should he wish it. The sea-reflecting blue eyes opposite him narrowed coldly for a moment before they closed in a bellow of laughter and the moment passed, like the rain outside. The sea was too uneasy, however, in the whipping wind to yield anything, but Bernard remembered one good story about his dead brother on a long-ago trip to Kinsale. Martin made a note in biro on the back of the wrist which held his fishing rod and Bernard knew it would be transferred to the mounting heaps of papers back at the hotel. More and more in the course of the programme he was being his own production assistant.

Mr O'Connor had carried in a mountain of turf for the fire and Eithne rather liked to listen to the rattle of the rain outside by way of contrast. Her hair was dry by now but spread all over the hearthrug and she swung it back in a tickling blanket over the recumbent John D who was still struggling with *The Irish Times* crossword.

"Give that over and sit up," she said, fetching her eternal dice-throwing version of Scrabble which she had bought somewhere in Holland.

"I was just going to work out another angle for that last shot to put to Martin when he gets back."

"Martin is probably half way to France by now on an ebbing tide. We'll find his pathetic little bits and pieces in the morning."

"Stop that!" John D was superstitious as well as red-haired. He was nervous about things like that. "All right, I'll give you three games and that's it."

"Nice John D. Did you notice Bernard's face today when you were strung up over the cliff, by the way?"

"I had other things to worry about. Is 'cadenza' allowed?"

"It's not English but I suppose it's in the OED like everything else – it's virtually been taken over, after all."

"OK, it's allowed." John D formed the word.

"But no *brio* or *allegro molto*," Eithne warned.

"No *brio* or *allegro molto* – I haven't the makings of them anyhow. What sort of look did Bernard have on his unlovely mug?"

"A bit nervous for you, I think. I think that's why he walked away."

"Arrogant bastard a lot of the time." John D swept up the dice after totting his score. "Are capitalists human? You should put that theme to Martin some time."

"More a Neville sort of line, surely? But I think you're wrong. He's shy and he's only just stopped being uneasy with us."

"Just in time to say goodbye then," said John D with satisfaction.

"There's hardly a week in it, if the weather lifts a bit."

"If," Eithne said, scooping a single good score. It was her game, her thing, but the others always won. "I think he's lonely, which only goes to show you money isn't everything."

"You can be miserable in much more comfort though. He looks to me like a bod who'd have it off wherever he pleased with one sex or t'other, despite his ugly mug. He has the brazen confidence you only get from too much money."

"I think you're wrong and the death of his brother is still bothering him after all these years. It's something I just have a hunch about. And then of course his wife walked out on him a few years ago. Prime bitch they say she was too. He came home one night and found not as much as a hair-clip left behind, and his baby gone too."

"'Hunch' is not a permissible word all the same.

Thirties slang," said John D with finality. "Why wouldn't she walk out on him when he's probably given to buggery?"

"It's much more permissable than "Cadenza". How about to hunch one's shoulders?"

"Go and ask Mr O'Connor if he has a dictionary then."

"You go. My hair isn't dry yet."

"Your hair is practically on fire, lady," John D said, settling himself comfortably on the hearthrug again. A car crunched in the sandy drive outside and Eithne gave a long sigh.

"Thank God. I couldn't have borne the smell of good country roast beef much longer."

"There'll be frogs' eyes to follow."

"At worst there'll be stewed apples, at best apple pie. Doesn't your nose tell you anything except whether a pint's good or bad?"

In out of the rain and the early dusk, Bernard was touched all over again by the sight of two apparent children playing a game beside the fire. He came over very willingly to join them when Eithne called and Martin went upstairs to look over his notes before dinner. He would call Evelyn on his way down, he said.

Later they all went out in the pouring rain to the pub and listened while a couple of local Carusos rendered songs like "Two Sweethearts" – one with hair of shining gold, the other with hair of grey – or the endless emigrant laments favoured by local taste. Whiskey chasing several pints made John D a bit quarrelsome and he shouted for a song from Bernard just to embarrass him. To everybody's surprise Bernard was not embarrassed. He stood up, supported only by two small Jamesons (the second of which he was still nursing) and gave the company a soft-voiced but not untuneful version of "Carrickfergus" which was vociferously applauded by the locals and earned him delighted approval from the team. Eithne thought they ought maybe incorporate "Carrickfergus" into the soundtrack, and John D wanted to know why they couldn't all move up to Carrickfergus and let Bernard do his party piece with his back against the castle walls. This suggestion was received with the contempt it deserved but Bernard wasn't discomfited.

That happened only when they got back to the guesthouse and he heard Martin telling Mrs O'Connor that they would almost certainly be finished shooting by the end of the week and would hardly stay over the weekend. The sinking of the heart was like what came long ago with the necessity of facing back to school after the long summer holidays. He felt ashamed of his emotion and unsure how to conceal it, so he went up early to his room. Normally they would hang about for hours yet, reading the newspapers they hadn't had time for during the day, swapping stories, doing crossword puzzles, discussing the next day's work. Usually he didn't contribute much to the conversation; like a silent member of a big family he was simply there, part of what was going on, perfectly content to sit up as long as they did.

Now there was something symbolic about hearing the murmur of their voices downstairs. The script had still to be written and there would be consultations in Dublin about it, hopefully with Martin, but (give or take a few days from now) the thing was over. Next week they would all be busy taking somebody else through his mental lumber-room. The little family would reform itself around another fire, and it would have nothing to do with him. And soon it would be April, breeding lilacs out of the dead land, mixing memory and desire. Time perhaps to go away; he had promised himself a few weeks in April. On the other hand, why not stay on here?

He let down the small dormer window and looked out over the water. This house echoed, in almost exact detail, that other, roofless, house; the murmur of voices, even, was like his sisters' voices before they settled down for the night, all together in the big back bedroom.

His own small room above the harbour used to be shared with his brother. The rain had stopped now and there was almost no sound from the sea and he wasn't surprised when Martin came to his door to say the weather forecast had been very good for the south-west and they might get in a full day's shooting tomorrow.

"Come in and have a nightcap," he invited, and Martin said he wouldn't stay long but happily didn't refuse the brandy when it was taken from the wardrobe.

"What will you do next?" Bernard asked, just for a moment unsure of how to begin.

"A bit of a break before I join Current Affairs for a short stint," the boy smiled. "Yours is the last programme in the present series. No more now until next season."

"You mean you're going to take a holiday?" He strove to make his voice sound casual, although he was suddenly aware of the beating of his heart.

"Unless something untoward crops up, yes."

212

"Why not join me in Greece, then, since that's where I'm heading next week or the week after? The place I have on Ios needs to be opened up after the winter and there's plenty of room, I assure you. Also two local women waiting to cook and clean for us." Bernard saw the refusal before it came; it was only a question of how it would be framed, how lightly he would be let down.

"It's a tempting offer, and there's nothing I'd enjoy more, all thing being equal. Never been further than Corfu as a matter of fact. But my wife has organised a resident babysitter for the two boys and we're off on a busman's holiday to Canada as soon as I'm free. Laura is Canadian you know. I met her when I was training in London with the BBC. When we get back, maybe you'd come over for supper with us some evening? Laura's an unpredictable cook, but you'll agree that doesn't matter too much when you meet her. Is it a deal?"

He drained the glass and got up off Bernard's bed with the same catspring, which was noticeable also in the way he walked.

"It's a deal. Many thanks. And maybe you'll both join me some time in Greece?"

Martin made the appropriate noises and didn't go at once, but started talking about a painter called Richard Dadd who (somebody had told him) had probably given Yeats his Crazy Jane themes. He hadn't seen the paintings himself at the Tate but Bernard had, so this kept them going until the door closed behind him, and on his youth, and on the hollow promise of knowing him as one knew every line of one's own hand. There was a lot of the night left and, fortunately, a lot of the brandy too.

The weather behaved as the weathermen said it would and the rest of the shooting went without a hitch. During this couple of weeks the year had turned imperceptibly towards summer, primroses in the land-facing banks, sea-pinks along the cliffs and an air about the television people that Bernard had seen before and couldn't quite place. Only when he went with them for the final day's shooting did he pin it down; a fairground the day after the circus. The television gear was more easily moved, of course; no long hours were needed for the pull-out. But the feeling was the same. They didn't believe him when he said he was staying on and they seemed shocked, which amused him, when he determinedly heaped presents on them the morning they were going: his Leica for Eithne who (incredibly) had never owned a camera of her own, a sheepskin jacket for John D because his own was in flitters from the rocks, a silver brandy flask (circa 1840), a cigarette lighter and a gold biro scattered apparently at random among the rest. The vulgarity of the largesse amused Bernard himself because such behaviour was not usual and he didn't entirely understand his impulse. But he understood perfectly why he gave Martin his signed first edition of *The Winding Stair*, a volume which for a year or more had lived in the right-hand door-pocket of his car for no better reason than that he liked to have it there. He had bought it somewhere along the quays in Cork.

> *Fair and foul are near of kin*
> *And fair needs foul,' I cried,*
> *'My friends are gone and that's a truth*

Nor grave nor bed denied
Learned in bodily lowliness,
And in the heart's pride.

A former owner had marked that with a small star in the margin, and Martin smiled slightly as he read it aloud in gratitude when the book fell open.

"I often have a disturbing feeling when I finish a job like this that I know – " he searched patiently for the words he wanted and his hesitation seemed to Bernard like comfort consciously-given for some loss he could understand. "That I know almost enough to begin all over again. Properly." He didn't smile at all when they shook hands so that the handgrip seemed warmer.

"Until soon, in Dublin," were his last words, a rather childish farewell which would have left a pleasant glow behind if Bernard had not known by now that they would not meet again.

The vanful of technology went on ahead of the boy's unreliable little red sports car, and watching from the drive of the guesthouse, Bernard had the feeling of the fairground again after the circus caravans have rolled away. It was peaceful, though, with the blue sea breathing quietly all around him and a few mares' tails of cloud slowly unravelling in the sky.

He was leaning over the wall considering how he would fill his remaining time when the guesthouse owner strolled by, indicating the blue boat which bobbed at the end of its mooring rope below them.

"You could take the aul' boat out fishing any day you had a fancy for it, Mr Golden. You're more than welcome to her any time though I wouldn't recommend today, mind you."

"I'm much obliged to you, Stephen. I have all the gear I need in the boot of the car so I might do just that. But why not today?"

"She'll rise again from the south-west long before evening," his host said positively. "And she'll blow herself out if I'm not mistaken. It would be a dangerous thing to go fishing out there today."

"The weathermen last night didn't mention any gales blowing up."

"The weathermen don't live around this Hook either," O'Connor said drily. "I've caught those same gentlemen out once or twice, and will again with the help of God."

"You might be right at that, I suppose. But if I do go out, I'll only fish for a short while, I promise you."

A pleasant man, Stephen O'Connor, a retired Civic Guard with an efficient wife to make a business out of the beautiful location of their house and her own hard work. Bernard remembered him vaguely from childhood, pedalling wet and fine around the coast roads, stopping here and there for a chat, missing nothing. It was he who had brought the news that Tom's body had been washed ashore somewhere near Kinsale. It was he who had in fact identified it. On remembering this Bernard toyed for a moment with the idea of having an actual conversation with this kindly man whose memories touched his own at one black juncture. The moment passed, however, and Stephen made a little more chat, lingering with natural courtesy just long enough for a guest to make up his mind whether or not further company would be welcome, and then he ambled contentedly in the direction of the greenhouse for the day's pottering. Old man, old man, if you never looked down again at a drowned face of my father's house it would be time enough for you. Forgive me, Stephen O'Connor.

The first warm sun of the year touched Bernard's eyes and he smiled, sitting up on the sea wall. No more Aprils, no more lilacs breeding out of the dead land, no more carnal awakenings. He felt peaceful, then a little surprised that the image behind his closed eyelids was not of his brother or of the young Martin or even of the caravans pulling out. It was the small wilful face of his daughter in the act of breaking away when one tried to hold her. He didn't know where she was, or even how she looked now, whether she still mirrored her mother in every gesture. He had a perfect right to know for the mere trouble of enforcing it. He hadn't done that, at first put off by the refusal of maintenance, by the eternal sound of the phone ringing in an empty flat and by two or three unanswered letters. He hadn't made a very energetic effort to keep in touch. As one year became two or three and now five, it had always seemed too late, but it would be untrue to pretend he greatly cared. It was just that, not being able to understand why the child's face should be so vivid in his mind, he was bothered by it as by some minor irritation, a door that slammed somewhere out of sight, a dripping tap. It wasn't until he was actually aboard the boat starting up the engine in a freshening breeze that he realised why he couldn't rid himself of his daughter's face today, of all days.

– fin –

451
Editions
www.451Editions.com